This book should be returned to any branch of the Lancashire County Library on or before the date shown

Lancashire County Library
Bowran Street
Preston PR1 2UX

Lancashire
County Council

www.lancashire.gov.uk/libraries

LL1(A)

Shadow Protector
JENNA RYAN

MILLS BOON

First published in Great Britain 2011
by Mills & Boon, an imprint of Harlequin (UK) Limited,
Large Print edition 2011
Eton House, 18-24 Paradise Road,
Richmond, Surrey TW9 1SR

© Jacqueline Goff 2010   **11774876**

ISBN: 978 0 263 21793 3

Harlequin (UK) policy is to use papers that are natural,
renewable and recyclable products and made from
wood grown in sustainable forests. The logging
and manufacturing process conform to the legal
environmental regulations of the country of origin.

Printed and bound in Great Britain
by CPI Antony Rowe, Chippenham, Wiltshire

JENNA RYAN

started making up stories before she could read or write. Growing up, romance alone always had a strong appeal, but romantic suspense was the perfect fit. She tried out a number of different careers, including modelling, interior design and travel, but writing has always been her one true love. That and her long-time partner, Rod.

Inspired from book to book by her sister Kathy, she lives in a rural setting fifteen minutes from the city of Victoria, British Columbia. It's taken a lot of years, but she's finally slowed the frantic pace and adopted a West Coast mindset. Stay active, stay healthy, keep it simple. Enjoy the ride, enjoy the read. All of that works for her, but what she continues to enjoy most is writing stories she loves. She also loves reader feedback. E-mail her at jacquigoff@shaw.ca or visit Jenna Ryan on Facebook.

To Samoa and Serendipity.
Part of the new Lucky Seven

Prologue

The dream unfolded piece by resistant piece in Serafina Hudson's sleeping mind.

She heard disembodied voices overlapping inside a viscous black fog. They murmured words like "death" and "danger" and "serial killer."

The mood altered. The voices grew louder. Fear slithered in, making the blackness cold.

Where was she? Sera wondered. Why couldn't she see?

"We look inside too much, Sera. That's our problem and our burden. It isn't all about the mind..."

Andrea's voice joined the mix. But that was impossible…

Because corpses couldn't speak!

Reality swept in, churning, swirling, spinning the black into blood red. Like the pool of blood her friend and colleague had been lying in on their office floor.

Sera remembered a slow, painful rise from dark to light. There'd been people everywhere, most of them wearing uniforms, all of them unfamiliar to her. Except for Len, the security guard. And Andrea.

Click into clinical mode. She was a doctor. She'd seen blood before.

Just not pooled around a body.

She swore three times. The hands vanished. Lights flashed red and blue. She'd be fine, a stranger promised. As for Andrea…

The voices stopped abruptly. The lights blurred. Her mind stuttered then seemed to wink out.

"Try to remember, Dr. Hudson…"

The mental prod repeated with an eerie echo. A man's face, hazy at first, solidified. He had creased, careworn features. He looked sixty and tough, yet she sensed an underlying kindness.

She also knew a cop when she saw one.

"I'm sorry your colleague's dead, Doctor. I wish I could change that, but I can't. Neither can you."

Had she thought the man was kind?

"You need to concentrate," he pressed. "We found a white bandanna at the murder scene. It's the signature of a serial killer. A phantom. You saw the person who did this—we're sure of it. You called Security. You screamed. The guard was down the hall, less than ten seconds away. He thought you were both dead when he found you…"

His voice trailed off. This really was a nightmare, Sera decided. Maybe if she did as the cop suggested and concentrated, she could erase some of the more gruesome aspects.

Determined, she willed the man away, shut

out the blurred lights and, because she knew it was important, concentrated on the throbbing pain at the base of her skull.

For a heartbeat, the world went dark.

When it relit, she was being ushered through a door. And, damn, there he was again. The care-worn cop.

"You'll be safe here, Doctor. Leo and I have been partners for twenty years. We haven't lost a witness yet."

She was a witness? Her mind snapped to attention. Had she seen Andrea's killer? Please, God, no, had she watched her die?

The walls and fixtures distorted. Two men spoke in the distance.

"Captain thinks there's a leak at headquarters, Leo. I agree with him."

"You're a pair of old ladies."

"She saw him. I know she did. If we can buy her enough time, she'll remember, and we'll have that bastard Blindfold Killer cold…"

The image of a white bandanna floated in. It fell over Andrea's lifeless, staring eyes.

Sera's mind gave a single convulsive shudder that had her surging upright in bed.

"Sera!"

The cop's voice cracked the night shadows like a whip. He caught her by the shoulders, held her steady and stared into her eyes. "Are you awake?"

Was she?

Sera's heart settled as the image of Andrea's rigid features faded.

"Yes." She breathed in, then out. "I had a nightmare."

"You only had the beginnings of one, Doc. Worst part's still to come."

Instinct had her bracing. "There's worse than my nightmare?"

"There's a leak in the department. I've suspected it for a while. I'm sure of it now. My partner's been killed. This place isn't safe."

Questions raced through Sera's head, too

many to ask. She wanted this to be part of her dream, but she knew it wasn't.

Two people were dead, and if the man who'd murdered them had his way, she'd be joining them. She'd been there the night he'd murdered Andrea. She'd seen his face.

All she had to do now was remember it.

Chapter One

"You're the psychiatrist, Doc. You tell me what's going on in this guy's pathetic excuse for a brain."

Sig Rayburn pushed on his forehead as if to compress his thoughts. Pain, worry, even a hint of fear had clouded his eyes during the two-day drive from San Francisco. The long, hot drive that currently had them blasting along Wyoming's I25 in his rusty brown Ford.

Sera searched for another vent. "Murderers usually have agendas, but that's not a given. I worked with a man once who liked watching people die. He said it gave him a buzz."

"Sexual?"

"Probably, although victim gender didn't matter. Neither did age or appearance." She paused, sat back, sighed. "Sig, where are we going?"

He pushed harder. "Tenth time you've asked me that since we left the motel this morning. I'm still not gonna tell you."

"Which says to me you don't know yourself, you think your car's bugged or you're weirdly superstitious. You're too good a cop to drive a bugged car, and you strike me as a man who always has a destination in mind, so I'll go with superstition and point out that wearing the same ratty T-shirt for three days straight at the safe house still didn't help the Giants win their series against the Dodgers."

"Got 'em close, though. Final game, eleventh inning. One little error in the outfield and poof, streak done."

The clouds rolled through his eyes again.

Reaching over, Sera squeezed his arm. "I'm really sorry about your partner's death."

"Not your fault, Doc. You didn't fire the bullet that took out the back half of his skull. Didn't slit your friend's throat either." He slanted her a speculative look. "You know who did, though. That's why we're doing this. You need time, distance and a safe place to unlock what's hidden inside that pretty head of yours. No offense," he added gruffly. "I know you have impressive credentials."

"None taken, and they're not as impressive as Andrea's were." Setting aside a twinge of guilt, Sera fanned her face with a Wyoming road map. "I'm pretty sure it won't jinx anything if you tell me our destination."

Sig waved at a buzzing fly. "You're wrong, Doc. Leo carried a lucky rock from Sedona the whole time we worked together. Kept it in his pocket with his loose change. When we found him in that alley, the change was there, but the rock wasn't. Don't talk to me about jinxes."

"Yes, but…"

"My nephew gave him that rock. Gave me one, too. Only time I left it behind, I took a bullet in my right calf."

"Where's your rock now?"

He jerked his head. "Backseat. Jacket pocket." When she didn't respond, he cocked a brow. "You think I'm nuts, don't you?"

"I don't analyze every idiosyncrasy, Sig."

"Uh-huh." But the challenge lingered. "You gonna tell me you don't have a quirk or two?"

"Oh, I have lots." She smiled. "But, no, I'm not going to tell you about them."

A rusty laugh preceded a gruff, "One thing's sure, Doc. Leo's gone, and he shouldn't be. No one better in the country at spotting or shaking a tail than him. Except…" With a glance at the distant Big Horn Mountains, he lapsed into silence.

Sera left him to his thoughts. His partner and friend was dead. Who better to understand how he felt than her? Even though…

She and Andrea hadn't been friends so much as friendly rivals. They'd known each other since they were five years old, but it was circumstance that had truly defined their relationship. Coincidence had also played its wily hand. From where they'd started—not a pretty picture—to where they'd ended up—as psychiatrists who'd obtained their degrees within months of each other—the outcome read like a small universal anomaly to Sera.

She closed her eyes and let the memories in. The murderer had left Andrea face up and staring at the shadowed ceiling. Through a swarm of police and medical workers, she'd looked like a broken doll—her skin chalk white, her features frozen in a mask of astonished horror.

Pain stabbed, swift and sure, and made her open her eyes.

"You're doing it again, aren't you?" Sig demanded. "Trying to smash down that wall in your brain."

She regarded the impressive peaks of the Big

Horns. "It's like I'm in an all-black room and there's a strobe light flashing at random intervals. I get split-second glimpses of things I don't understand, then it's back to black, and I want to scream, because no matter how hard I try, I can't make sense of them."

"Could be you're trying too hard."

She slid him a vaguely humorous look. "Your name's Rayburn, right, not Freud?"

"What, you've never said that to a patient?"

"Not any more."

Sig went back to pushing on his forehead while Sera contemplated the landscape. The scenery was magnificent, as was the clear, blue sky. July in Wyoming was all about pine forests, spectacular mountain ranges and wide-open vistas that possessed a beauty all their own.

She felt a tease on the edge of her brain and tipped her head from side to side in an effort to center it. One image, that's all she needed to extract. Unfortunately, research suggested that forcing a resistant memory tended to be as effective as striking a nail with a feather.

She watched a pair of hawks glide in a wide arc beneath a cloudless stretch of sky.

"What's that look for?" Sig asked.

"I have a look?"

"Like you'd rather be riding a cable car."

A smile tugged on her lips. "My face isn't that readable, Detective."

"Hell it isn't. You're sleek, sophisticated and polished. You probably wear high heels to the grocery store. I don't mean to sound patronizing, but I have to warn you, where we're headed, the only place you'll see five stars is in the night sky."

Sera's smile widened. "Putting on your bad cop hat, huh?"

"Doc, you haven't seen anything like bad yet. When we get—aw, hell, what's this?"

"It sounds like a siren."

"Was I speeding?"

"Unless the limit's upward of ninety, yes."

"Crap." He slowed and pulled over.

The officer who approached the car did so with long, easy strides. He rested a forearm on the roof while Sig stretched back to snag the jacket behind him.

"Is there a problem, Officer?"

"Not unless you make one. Got your license with you?"

"Got better than that." Sig fished in the pocket, handed Sera what she assumed was his lucky rock and produced his badge with a flourish.

"San Francisco, huh?"

She caught a trace of humor in the other cop's drawl. His surprisingly sexy drawl, she thought. As for his features, she couldn't see them under the brim of his hat.

She knew he glanced at her before pushing off. "Out of the car, please, Detective Rayburn."

"Have I done something wrong?"

"Depends how fast you get out of the car."

"Don't move," Sig told her. He had to shove twice on the door to open it. "You're starting to piss me off here, Officer. I'm a detective with the San Francisco Police Department, homicide division. Who are you to be ordering me around like a common criminal?"

Sera saw the flash of a surprisingly attractive smile. "I clocked you at ninety-six miles an hour as you flew past Moss Creek."

Sig's balled right fist drew an even wider smile. A second later, her companion went from a short punch on the other cop's shoulder to a backslapping hug.

It figured. Sera breathed out but couldn't bring herself to be annoyed. It was such a predictable male game.

"I'm damn glad to see you, Logan." Sig drew back, grinned. "How'd you know? License plate give me away?"

The taller man glanced from side to side. "This isn't a car, Sig—it's dented metal on wheels. One of a kind." Without looking or pausing, he asked, "Does she know?"

Sig shook his head.

That did it. Shouldering her door open, Sera slid out. "Excuse me, gentlemen, but 'she' has a name. It's Sera, and the reason she doesn't know is because the man with the San Francisco badge refuses to tell her anything."

"It's for your own…"

"Protection. Got that one yesterday, Sig. But six diners, five gas stations and one truly crappy motel later, I think I've earned the right to know not only where we're going, but also why a police officer in another state is better informed than I am." She sent them a placid smile over the roof of the car. "If it's not too much trouble."

Apart from his badge and the lights on his Explorer, nothing about the man in front of her said law enforcement officer. He wore jeans and a short-sleeved black T-shirt. His boots were dusty, his hat was decidedly more cowboy than cop and if he was carrying a gun, Sera couldn't see it.

Sig matched her smile as he turned to his friend. "Handful," he said.

"See that," the man replied. He nodded forward. "Nadine'll be serving dinner about now. Her place is on the edge of town. You can follow me." Although his eyes were shielded, Sera felt his gaze across the top of the car. "Nadine runs her grandfather's diner, Dr. Hudson. You can ask your questions while we eat." Nudging his hat forward so the brim hid the entire upper portion of his face, he added, "Assuming once they're answered, you still want to eat."

She wouldn't react, Sera promised herself. That would be counterproductive. Instead, she let Sig concentrate on the road that wound away from the interstate through a majestic expanse of pines, boulders the size of city buildings and a steady stream of out-of-state trucks.

Five miles in, the truck traffic thinned, the boulders softened and houses began to appear. Farmhouses at first, followed by larger, turn-of-the-century homes that ambled back from tree-lined streets.

A rustic sign with a hand-carved mountain

peak rising above a lake welcomed them to Blue Ridge, Home of the Happy Mountaineer. Population five thousand, six hundred and twenty-seven.

Sig glanced in the rearview mirror. "Do you see my smokes back there?"

"No, and I'm not digging through a pile of old food wrappers and napkins to find them. You're a rolling health hazard, Detective Rayburn. Cigar stubs, cigarette butts and God knows how many million bacteria, all alive and thriving inside your vehicle. You inhale coffee like air, pour enough grease into your arteries to kill an elephant and probably haven't gotten eight hours of smoke-free sleep since you joined the force."

He chuckled. "You're a shrink, Sera. What does a head doctor know about high cholesterol, lung disease and sleep deprivation?"

She lifted the dark hair from her neck. "Among other things, my uncle does a week-end medical clinic in Haight-Ashbury. I help out when he needs it, which is often because he tends to be overrun and doesn't like to turn anyone away. How do you know him, Sig?" she asked after a brief pause. "The cop with the…" She started to say sexy mouth but changed it to "…black hat?"

He peered into the setting sun. "Oh, Logan and me go way back." A finger tapped the windshield. "Is he pulling off the road? All I can see is dust."

"Gravel parking lot." She let her hair fall. "My skin hates you."

"Your skin's gorgeous, as, I trust, are your manners. Five stars…"

"Yes, I know. Only in the night sky. As long as the food's recognizable, I'm good."

And more than ready to stop, she realized, stretching her back as she slid from the car seat.

Every article of clothing she wore, from the pale-green linen halter to the white capris stuck to some part of her body. And it was going to be an adventure navigating the unpaved, pothole-filled parking lot in strappy three-inch heels.

A collection of trucks and SUVs sat at odd angles outside the weather-beaten one-story building whose sign read Frank's Diner.

She stopped stretching to do a humorous double take down the side. "Are those horses?"

"The bay's Billy the Kid. The black is Jesse James."

She suppressed an urge to jump when the cop in jeans wrapped his fingers around her arm.

"Nadine's grandfather swears one of his ancestors was related to Jesse."

"So he named a horse after him."

She caught the quirk of his lips in profile. "No one you know's ever been named for a dead relative?"

"Not a notorious one, Officer…"

"Leave it at Logan."

"Evening, Chief. Rain's coming." The man shambling past, sprinkling tobacco in a rolling paper, barely spared them a glance. "It's my night for poker if you feel like letting us win back some of our hard-earned cash. Wouldn't blame you a mite, though, if not. She's a real pretty lady."

Sera would have grinned if she hadn't caught the edge of a rut and almost snapped her ankle in two.

"Horses, poker and holes big enough to swallow small children. I'm charmed…" She cast the man who'd caught her a sideways look. "Chief."

"It's a label. Means nothing."

"Uh-huh. It only signifies that you're in charge of a town containing five thousand, six hundred and twenty-seven souls. Which would make sense at this point in Sig's life. But everything about you screams big city cop to me."

His lips quirked again. "You might want to check your inner voice, Doc. Cities and me don't get along these days."

Meaning they had once? Interesting, she reflected, as they reached the diner's porch. But it wasn't as interesting as the fact that he knew her name and undoubtedly her story.

Several feet behind them, Sig sucked smoke

into his lungs at an alarming rate. Because her arm was tingling, Sera eased free and strove for an unimpeded look at the man called Logan.

He was tall and rangy, with sleek muscles, long legs and dark hair that curled well below the back of his hat. He needed a cut and a shave. And she needed distance because not only was her skin tingling, but also her pulse was doing an erratic tap dance.

Food would help, she decided, plucking at the front of her top. "Is Nadine a good cook?"

"Best down home in Blue Ridge."

"He means if you're expecting art on a plate, you won't get it here." Sig studied the black clouds massing over the distant Big Horns. "Those coming this way?"

"Joe says they are. He's usually right."

"Then we should get down to business."

Sera arched guileless brows. "We're doing business? I thought we stopped here for answers and a hearty meal."

"I'm stopping, Doc. Got something different in mind for you."

Where was a control button when you needed one?

"Sig..."

"You're not stopping, Sera. You're staying."

Prepared for that response, she met his hard stare and simply asked, "Why?"

"Because I trust Logan. He's the best, and as bad as I wanted that bastard Blindfold Killer before, I want him doubly bad now. He's murdered sixteen people over the years. That includes his most recent victims, your friend and my partner. You saw his face, Doc. I know it, and so do you. Unfortunately—and this is where my faith in Logan comes in—one hell of a vicious killer knows it, too."

Chapter Two

"Your captain told me about the Blindfold Killer, Sig," Sera said. "No one's sure why he ties a white bandanna over his victims' eyes. He's killed eleven people over a seven-year period, all in the Bay area. The San Francisco Police arrested a suspect four years ago, but they were forced to release him on a technicality."

"Illegal search of his living quarters," Logan said. "The officer in charge assumed a warrant was en route. He was mistaken."

"Said officer has since been demoted and put in charge of a desk," Sig added gruffly. Then he brightened. "Ah, here we go. Food."

Their dinner arrived courtesy of a buxom fifty-something blonde. It might not be gourmet, but it looked delicious. Almost as delicious as the man seated across from her.

Although she'd braced herself for sexy, Sera hadn't anticipated the punch of desire that had rocked her when he'd removed his hat.

And then, out of nowhere, a tweak of familiarity. But the sensory whisper came and went too quickly for her to capture it.

Sidestepping, she set her mind back on the man himself. To call his features arresting would be a serious understatement. And she couldn't imagine any woman not being wowed by the smoke-gray eyes that caught and held hers far too often for comfort.

One look at Logan's face, however, and she'd known he wouldn't be an easy read. Whatever haunted those mesmerizing features, he'd buried it deep and very, very well.

Sig dug into his steak. "What else do you know about our killer, Doc?"

Refocusing quickly, Sera sampled one of the wedge fries. "Two and a half years went by after the suspect's release. Nothing more happened. Then he vanished, and it started all over again. The killer has committed five new murders, including Leo, in the past eighteen months. His MO is consistent, but his motive remains a mystery."

When Andrea's lifeless face appeared in her head, Sera reached for her wine.

"There've been two witnesses to his crimes. Number one vanished five years ago, before the police could bring him in. That makes me the best hope you've got of identifying this guy. Unfortunately, because I hit my head while I was struggling with him, I can't tell you if his description matches the original suspect's or not."

Logan swirled his beer and sent a lazy look into the mug. "You don't remember the guy's face, but you do remember struggling with him."

Surprise halted the wine at her lips. The image

reformed instantly. "He blindsided me," she recalled. "I fell against the edge of my desk."

"Anything else?" Sig asked.

She thought for a moment but couldn't pull any details from the blackness. "Sorry, the rest is still a shadow."

Around them, the diner, really a roadside bar and grill, began to buzz as groups of dusty workers in steel-toed boots filed in.

Sig tapped an unlit cigarette on the table. "New construction in town?"

With his eyes on Sera's face, Logan took a drink of beer. "West end. Developer from Cheyenne's building a—resort."

The amusement that climbed into Sera's throat felt good. "Translation—he's building a resort-style fishing and hunting lodge."

Sig tucked a pack of matches into his jacket pocket and scraped his chair back. "I can't think in the throes of a nicotine fit." He gave Sera's arm an awkward pat. "Keep poking at that memory, Doc. This killer's slick and slippery and far as we can tell random in his selection of victims. Logan." Cigarettes in hand, he made his way through the crowd toward the door.

"He didn't finish his dinner," Sera remarked.

Logan speared one of her fries. "Sig seldom finishes any meal that doesn't start with the prefix Mac."

"How old is he?"

"Fifty-six."

"He acts older."

"Drawn-out investigations do that to cops."

Leaning in on her forearms, she absorbed his unfathomable stare. "I'm sure I've seen…" she began, but the fleeting sense of familiarity vanished again. "Is that why you left?" she asked instead.

"Nope."

Door firmly closed. She picked up her wine. "How long have you been in Blue Ridge?"

"Two years, three months, give or take."

"And you became chief of police when?"

"Same answer."

Pulling teeth would be easier, she reflected, but nowhere near as challenging.

"How long have you known Sig?"

"Longer than most."

"You're not giving me much in the way of answers, Logan."

His gray eyes glittered. "Should tell you something about the questions."

Undeterred, she ran a finger around the base of her glass. "You don't like small talk or, apparently, polite conversation. No problem. I don't need to know your history, and you certainly don't need to know mine." She made a visual circle of the increasingly noisy diner. "This whole take-the-witness-with-the-faulty-memory to Wyoming deal was Sig's idea. It had nothing to do with me. I have relatives in Phoenix, Skagway, Tulsa and yes, Bugs, even Albuquerque. I have a cousin who's a law enforcement officer and an ex-military aunt who flies supplies from Washington state to central Alaska. I could have gone to any number of people for help, but I went with Sig and wound up here. Why? No idea, but hey, you put your life in someone else's hands, who knows what'll happen."

"Are you done?" Logan asked.

"My uncle Jeffrey says I'm never done, but as a shrink, I'm supposed to be a good listener, so the floor's yours."

He held her gaze. "What you're supposed to be—what you should be, Sera—is scared."

She summoned a faint smile, glanced away. "Believe me when I tell you, if I wasn't, I wouldn't be anywhere near you, your outlaw horses or your town." A shiver danced along her spine. "Nothing personal, Logan, but I get along very well with cities. Violent death, however, rattles me. I watched my partner's ashes being entombed last week. I watched her father break down and her mother lose a hard-fought battle to a bottle of cognac. I saw Sig lose a friend he's worked with for twenty of his thirty years on the force. I did all that with the knowledge that

lurking somewhere in my head is a killer's identity. If I can retrieve it, no one else will have to
suffer at his hands. So, yes, I'm scared, but not
as much as I am determined to watch the person
who's responsible—and whose face I swear I'm
going to remember—fry."

Unexpected humor glinted in Logan's eyes.
"You must have some outlaw blood yourself,
Doc. I've never met a shrink who wanted to see
anyone fry."

Her first reaction was to defend the remark.
Her second was to cover a smile with a bite of
chicken. "I won't tell you what my uncle says
about my mouth. I will tell you I'm sorry I
dumped all that on you when we've known each
other for less than sixty minutes."

He moved a shoulder. "Dumping's what
people do on cops, town, city or state. It rolls off
unnoticed after a while… Nadine?" He spoke to
the blonde who was balancing six main courses.
"You mind wrapping these dinners up for us?"

Sera's brows elevated. "Are we leaving?"

"Unless you want to get hit on by every guy here, yeah."

For the first time since Sig had gone outside, she looked around the room. Not every male eye was turned in their direction, but more than half were.

She let the amusement blossom. "Because I assume they're not staring at you, I'll go out on a limb and speculate that you don't get many female strangers in this town."

Logan picked up his hat. "Oh, we get plenty of strange females, just not many you'd call witchy."

The blonde returned with their bagged dinners. "You want the steak wrapped, too, Logan?"

He finished his beer. "No point. Give your dogs a treat, and put the dinner on my tab."

The woman flipped a dishtowel over her shoulder. "Your friend beat you to the punch there. He paid the bill on his way out."

Something unpleasant snaked through Sera's

stomach. Although she recognized it for the blend of dread and certainty it was, she settled for a mild, "He's gone, isn't he?"

Logan assessed her as he returned the hat to his head. "He told you he wasn't staying, Sera."

"And I'm just supposed to go with that? With this?" She fixed her gaze in the general vicinity of his eyes. "With you? No questions asked or really answered, and no choice in the matter?" Her control slipped a notch and she leaned forward. "Logan, Sig broke a mirror at the safe house and freaked over it for days. We were driving east within an hour of his partner's death. 'Gotta leave fast,' he said. Yet, he went ten minutes out of his way because he wouldn't go past the path lab where his partner's body had been taken. Said he'd rather walk under a dozen ladders. He also didn't tell anyone in the department where we were going, and I know his captain personally. He's a forty-year man with commendations as long as my arm."

"What's your point, Doctor?"

Did she have one? Right then, Sera's thoughts were too scattered to collect, let alone organize.

It had to be exhaustion combined with a touch of hysteria that made her want to laugh. "You know what?" She pushed back. "I haven't got a clue what I'm saying or why I'm even talking. I need air, space and no more Willie Nelson for at least twelve hours."

She also needed to be away from the man across the table. The ridiculously sexy cop who disliked cities and personal questions and quite possibly his old friend Sig at this moment.

Standing, Logan drew her to her feet. "You look over-whelmed."

"You think?"

"If it helps, Sig left your bags behind my truck."

"Sorry, Chief, not feeling any better here."

The shadowed look he cast her brought a sigh coupled with a strong desire to bolt.

"Okay, fine. Message received. Sig's trying to keep me safe, as a person and as a potential witness. What I'm still trying to process is why he brought me to you. He talked about a potential leak within the department, but please don't tell me he suspects his own captain."

"Twenty years in homicide, ten in vice, what can I say, he's jaded."

"You sure you don't mean paranoid?"

Pressing a hand to her hip, Logan eased her behind him as he forged a path to the door. "Sig's a cautious man, Sera. He wants to keep you alive, and this was the best place he could think of to make that happen."

A man with no bottom teeth winked and offered her his drink.

Logan's unruffled, "Doctor, Billy," had the leer fading to a scowl and the man scuttling backward so fast he almost knocked the plates from Nadine's loaded arm.

Sera tapped his back. "Care to explain that reaction?"

"Billy's father turned ninety-eight last June.

Doc Prichard said he needed a vitamin shot. The old man died that night."

"Uh—well, hmm." Unsure how to respond, Sera tried not to grin. "Ninety-eight, huh? Billy doesn't really believe it was the vitamin shot—" She let an oblique hand motion finish the question. "Does he?"

"Yeah, he does, and he's not alone. Most of the people you'll meet around here are perfectly normal, but for every fifty, there's a Billy or a Jessie-Lynn. Rumor has it aliens grabbed Jess twelve years ago after the Founder's Day parade." Logan opened the door—and closed it in the face of a large, hairy man whose hand had been mere inches from Sera's breast.

Removing his hat, he placed it on her head and smiled just enough to momentarily steal her breath. "I hate to be the bearer of bad news, Dr. Hudson, but you're not in Kansas any more. And while you might think the Emerald City is a little off the map—be warned, it has nothing on Blue Ridge, Wyoming."

HE SHOULDN'T HAVE said that, Logan thought as he started his Explorer. But, dammit, he didn't want the burden of a targeted witness's safety riding on his shoulders. Add in the fact that she was a jaw-dropping female of—what had Sig told him—twenty-nine, with credentials that shouldn't be possible for someone her age and a body just made for trouble, and yeah, you could say he was pissed off. Mostly at himself for re-acting the way he was, but partly at Sig for put-ting him in this position.

He knew she didn't remember him. Why would she? They'd never met face to face. Their one and only patch of common ground involved the age-old cop versus shrink battle. Was the suspect the police had arrested for a brutal crime fit to stand trial or not? On their particu-lar patch, a trio of shrinks, whose number had included Sera, said no.

Now, the way Logan saw it, he could let old resentments fester or, for Sig's sake, put the past in its place and deal with the current situation.

One glance at her face in profile, and he knew where he'd be going with that.

Although she had to know his thoughts weren't running along pleasant lines, she opted to keep their conversation relevant and, for the most part, impersonal.

"The suspect was under surveillance when he disappeared, wasn't he?" she asked.

Logan shoved the Explorer in gear and his emotions in line. "His name's Hugh Paxton, and yes, he was. He dropped out of sight a few months after I came to Blue Ridge."

She regarded him from under the brim of his hat. "Did you hear about that from Sig, or did your alien abductee return from the mother ship a gifted clairvoyant?"

Humor stirred. "Jessie-Lynn has her moments, but the answer's no on both counts. Remote as this town is, we have a local newspaper, and believe it or not, Internet access."

Pushing the hat back, she lowered her sunglasses. "I'm not a snob, Logan, whatever you might think—and God knows it probably isn't flattering. I'm just a little—no make that a lot—out of my element here. I don't usually see horses grazing outside San Francisco diners, and unless we wander into the wrong area of the city, big, hairy men seldom make a habit of grabbing women's breasts."

"So, no conquest for Charlie, then. He'll be bummed."

She laughed, and the sound of it sparked a sensation Logan didn't need to feel in his groin. Keeping his eyes on the road, he returned to topic. "Paxton walked because the arresting officer screwed up, but he was the Blindfold Killer. Every cop on the coast knew it."

Sera regarded the dying orange glow in the western sky. "He'd have known the police were watching him, ergo, for a while at least, his desire for freedom must have outweighed his need to kill. Either that or he'd achieved his initial goal of eleven people dead. It's possible his more recent victims are unconnected to the first group."

"No one ever established a connection between the first eleven victims." Logan chose to ignore the out-of-town driver who whizzed past in a mud-spattered four by four. "Any thoughts on that, Doc?"

"Without getting inside his head, no." But as he'd expected, after a moment she ventured to ask, "Were the victims primarily female or male?"

"Eight female, three male."

"Ages?"

"The youngest was twenty, the oldest forty-seven."

"And Paxton's age at the time of his arrest was?"

A smile touched the corners of Logan's mouth. "That's the sticking point. No one knows. He has no official record of birth and the kind of appearance every cop hates."

"Changeable?"

"Big time."

"Which explains why Sig showed me multiple versions of ten different men, more than a hundred shots in total. I figured there were disguises involved—but, big surprise—Sig refused to explain. He said the less he told me, the less chance that my memories, when they did return, would be colored. All he really needed to say was that the suspect took his cue from Lon Chaney."

Logan sent her a brief smile. "It's not a bad comparison. Twenty pounds more or less, from dreadlocks to buzz cuts, stubble to mustache to beard, tooth caps on or off, contact lenses in or out—Paxton knows how to alter his appearance. It's one of the reasons he was so difficult to nail in the first place. The other was the obvious lack of credible witnesses."

"I assume that's how he slipped under the radar. In disguise."

When the radio squawked, Logan reached down. "Probably, but I was gone by then, and

Sig was so disgusted that they'd lost him, he wouldn't talk about it."

Her eyes slid to his, but she said nothing, and he pressed the Receive button. "Problem, Fred?"

"The Bulley boys are at it again, Chief."

"Home or town?"

"Home now, but they came through town on a big old tear. Near as I can tell, they're riled up over the workers who are camped out—quite legally, I might add—on their farm. Did some pushing and shoving on Main, went into Tommy Gray Wolf's bar, had a shouting match, punched someone, then took off for home when Tommy threatened to call it in. Which he did anyway ten minutes before Edgar Bulley did the same. Old Edgar says there's no point sending deputies. The boys'll just threaten to gore them and carry on 'til you show up."

Logan glanced over. "I'll be there in five. Tell Edgar to fire a couple rounds of buckshot into the barn wall. Might take the edge off."

"Always a first time," Fred returned cheer-fully. "Good luck, Logan."

As the sun dipped below the mountaintops, he switched on the lights and siren. "How are you at following orders, Doc?"

She dropped his hat on the seat between them. "The mood I'm in, spectacularly bad. Did I hear the word 'gore'?"

"It's the Bulley's word for 'stab.' Used to be a kid's game involving plastic horns. Now it's a drunken threat when they're feeling ornery."

"Sounds like your Bulley boys have serious anger management issues."

"You could say," he agreed. "Their grandfa-ther grazes a stingy herd of cattle, but the num-ber's been dwindling over the years, so the boys, six of them, have been forced to find other ways to augment their income."

"Ways you *smoke* or *drink?*"

"Drink mostly. We've dismantled three stills since late March. Last one was five days ago. Supply's probably running low, so Bulley logic would dictate that they down the last of it and take their anger out on someone else."

"Like deputies and campers."

"They've also been known to fire warning shots at trespassers." Logan slowed as the lights of a ramshackle farmhouse came into view. "Challenge is to see how close they can come without actually hitting the person. Fortunately," he flicked off the siren, "they're not in love with firearms. Knives tend to be their weapon of choice."

Braking behind a stand of pines, he reached for his rifle, stuck the hat back on his head and caught her chin between his thumb and fingers. "Whatever happens, Sera, keep the doors locked and the engine running. Anyone who isn't me shows up, don't check for blood, just turn the truck around and head back to Frank's Diner. You got that?"

"Every word," she said. "Uh, tell me, are two of the Bulley boys tall, wiry and left-handed?"

A brow went up when her eyes touched on a point over his shoulder. "Coming from behind?"

"Faster than speeding bullets."

Anticipation glimmered. Releasing her chin, he reached for the door handle. "This is gonna be fun."

Chapter Three

"Logan?" As amused as she was amazed, Sera worked her way over the console to the driver's seat. She stared into the rapidly expanding darkness. "Forget Jesse James. Houdini must be one of your ancestors."

No matter which direction she looked, she couldn't see him. He was gone, and so were the two men. Obviously they'd vanished into the trees, but talk about witchy people—this place had it all over San Francisco—and that was saying a lot.

She was searching for the lock control when a face popped up at the driver's side window. A split second later the door flew open and a pair of grimy hands, one of them wielding a knife, shot inside.

Startled, Sera jumped back. She gave the passenger door a shove and the man's wrist a kick.

Spying Logan's gun, she grabbed it and tumbled from the truck.

It was hardly surprising that her heels unbalanced her and she landed on the ground. But she didn't spend three nights a week at the gym for nothing. She was on her feet before the man could wriggle through the interior.

His lips peeled back when he got his first good look. "Hoo-ee, you are a pretty thing, aren't you, baby doll?"

On her feet now, Sera raised the gun. "Don't make me shoot," she told him. "I don't want to hurt you."

He hopped out, snickering when her hand trembled. "You sure you got the right end pointed at me?"

"Do you want to find out?"

He didn't stop completely, but she saw him hesitate. He was drooling, she noticed. And limping slightly.

She kept her arm extended, and flicked her gaze down then back to his face. "How old were you when you broke your right leg?"

Shock halted him in a way the gun hadn't. "How'd you know about that? You Jessie-Lynn's cousin from Casper?"

"No, I'm…"

"A witch then." His already small eyes narrowed. "Gramps says there's a bunch of them living up Buffalo way."

"He means Wiccans."

"Don't matter what he means. How'd you know about my leg?"

"It wasn't set right so the bone didn't heal properly. I'm guessing you were young and still growing. Maybe ten or eleven?"

"Twelve." His lip curled. "You a doctor?"

"Yes."

He made a sound of disgust and spit to the side.

Sera kept her tone and expression calm. "I see."

"You're a jackass like Prichard."

"Only on weekends in Haight-Ashbury. Don't make me shoot," she said again when he lurched forward.

The snarl became a sneer. "Doctors don't go round shooting people, now do they, baby doll? Anyway, I think you're lying. Saw me limping, took a lucky guess."

Still fifteen feet away, Sera could smell the alcohol on his breath. He whipped out a taunting arm, then laughed and feinted forward.

Double handing the gun, Sera put pressure on the trigger. "You really don't want me to do this."

"Want it more than you do, I figure. Come on, baby, show Benny what you got."

When he moved again, she fired. Missed him

by several feet, but the shock of it had him hopping backward.

"You ain't no doctor, lady…" Then he stopped. "You ain't no kind of shot either." His eyes gleamed as he recovered lost ground. "Grab her, Danny."

She heard a twig crack. Waiting a beat, she plowed her elbow into the stomach of the man behind her, then spun away to fire a second shot. The bullet thwacked off a tree. From her knees—when had she lost her footing—she squeezed again.

The Bulley with the bruised stomach bared his teeth.

Sera knew she couldn't win this. Both men were advancing, both were drunk and she had a feeling it was the heel of her shoe snapping off that had landed her on the ground.

"Looks like we got a she-cat on our hands, Benny," the bigger Bulley growled. "How 'bout I…"

The rest of his sentence emerged in a whoosh

of air as he hit the tree behind him with enough force to send him slithering down the trunk.

Swinging around, Logan used the butt end of his rifle on the other man's jaw. Benny pivoted in a slow half circle before dropping like felled timber.

"Might want to take your time getting up," Logan suggested. His eyes were on Sera as he spoke. Holding out a hand, he drew her to her feet. "You hurt?"

"No more than if I'd been working out with Hulk Hogan in his prime." She waved the tip of his gun between the two prone men. "Do you do this sort of thing often then?"

"Often enough." Raising his voice, he said, "Lloyd and Jake are cooling off in the barn. They were smart enough to ditch their knives when they spotted me."

"Didn't mean no harm, Logan." Benny's words were muffled by the dirt beneath his face.

"You threatened the lady with a weapon. It's

called intent. On your feet, both of you, and into my truck."

"Come on, Lo…" But one look and Benny dropped his face back into the dirt. "Yeah, sure, whatever you say."

Danny worked himself into a squat. "I'm supposed to be stocking shelves at the grocery store tonight, Logan. Miguel won't be happy with you."

Ignoring him, Logan indicated the gun in Sera's hand. "I hope you pointed that a good long way off target."

"I did. Here." She handed it over.

"Her bullet came closer to my crotch than my knife did to any part of her," Benny called out. "Maybe I wanna press charges myself. Against you for bringing her here and her for almost shooting my balls off."

"Right." Sera extended her hand. "Give it back."

Logan grinned. "He's just pissed because he's going to be spending a couple nights in jail."

She wiggled her fingers. "Give it. I promise, I won't shoot them."

Clearly intrigued, he relinquished the weapon.

"Hey, wait a minute," Benny spluttered.

"Don't move," Sera said and, taking aim, sent one of the pebbles on the ground between his spread feet zinging into the bushes behind him.

AN AMUSED LOGAN said little on the drive into town. That was fine with Sera. After changing her shoes, she climbed into his truck and let Etta James drown out the Bulley boys' gripes.

Apparently, the police chief planned for her to stay in his home. It made sense, but it hardly set her mind at ease. The more time she spent with him, the stronger the feeling that she should know him.

They hadn't met—she'd have remembered that in a minute. Seen his name then? Possibly. She could see it well enough on the lighted dash.

Michael Richard Logan. And, ding, there went

another bell. Had her memory been more com-
promised than she realized?

Unable to answer that, she returned to the
moment.

The Bulleys' grumbles grew louder the closer
they got to Blue Ridge. Inside the station, Logan
handed them over to his deputy, Toby, a young
man with bright red hair. "Separate cells," he
said and tossed the young man the keys.

The deputy looked like he'd rather drink ar-
senic. "Uh, Logan, er, Chief, I'm not sure—I
mean, they're my cousins. I can't just, you know,
put them behind bars."

Logan searched through a drawer. "Don't
sweat it, Toby. You're only the messenger."

"But don't messengers get shot sometimes?"

"Hang around here long enough, you'll get
shot one way or another," Danny Bulley snarled.
"Do what you gotta, Toby. Just know you won't
be getting no freebies for a good long while." At
Logan's raised brow, he added, "Dinners."

All in all, Sera spent less than fifteen minutes

at the station. Ten more, and they were pull-ing up outside a very old, very large house that Logan informed her had come with the job.

Sera sensed his stare as he removed her bags from the back of his truck. With her skin prick-ling, she swung to confront him.

"What?" she demanded and received the kind of slow smile she really didn't need to see right then. "Is it the gun?"

"Yeah, but it can wait until we're inside."

As he spoke, a drop of rain from clouds she'd failed to notice plopped onto her head.

"You've got about five seconds to decide… or not," he amended when the night sky simply opened up.

If this had been San Francisco and she'd been going to work, Sera would have run. But here, in the middle of nowhere, with the lights of town a distant blur and her clothes already streaked with dirt, she simply lifted her face to the warm rain.

"I have to tell you, Logan, this qualifies as one

of the strangest days of my life, and I've had some really bizarre days."

He set his hat back on her head and picked up the heavy bags. "Courtesy of your patients?"

"Not even close."

Hoisting her carryall, laptop and purse, she preceded him up a short walk to a porch that appeared to wrap around the entire farmhouse. She counted three floors, plus an L-shaped jut and an attic.

Lamps burned in three of the first floor windows. A dog barked deep inside.

"Her name's Ella Fitzgerald. She's a two-year-old golden retriever who thinks she's a lap dog. Can you handle that?"

She smiled. "I love dogs."

"Good, now how are you with…"

The door opened before he could finish and a small, thin woman with a frizzy gray bun whisked them inside.

She looked cranky, made rough tutting noises

and, with a single sharp look, held them on the hallway mat.

"Moon Flower." Logan caught the towels she tossed from the closet. "Also came with the job."

"Use it." The woman pointed downward. "I waxed the floors today."

"Yes, ma'am."

"Call me Flo. You'd be Dr. Hudson, then. Sit, Ella. Her room's ready, like you wanted, Logan—the one across from yours. If you have a moment, Doctor, my sister's foot's been troubling her. And before you ask, she drinks plenty of milk."

Sera had no idea what to say. "I'm uh, glad to hear it."

Logan hung their towels on the doorknob and removed the dripping hat from her head. "She's not that kind of doctor, Flo, and she's not here to work in any case."

"I see. Fine then. Babe can just hobble around until that knot head who calls himself an MD decides to practice human rather than simian medicine. Room's this way, Doctor."

"Sera's good."

"You know, Babe can hardly walk some days. Doesn't matter how much milk she drinks."

"Phone's ringing, Flo." Logan nodded into the living room. "I'll take Sera upstairs." When the woman bustled off, he said, "Don't ask. She was part of the original hippie movement. She lived in a bus for three years. The engine died after one. She met my dispatcher Fred thirty-seven years ago. They got high, got married and started their own business in Sacramento."

"Would that be a hemp shop?"

He indicated a set of stairs that jogged to the right halfway up. "Fencing mainly, and not the white picket kind."

"So thirty some years later, it's only natural they'd be working for the chief of police in a northern Wyoming town."

"Life meanders, Sera. Why don't you tell me your shoot-'em-up story?"

Wet and dirty, with a big dog nosing her hip and a too-sexy man on the stairs behind her, Sera opted for the abbreviated version.

"An adopted aunt whose father was a Texas Ranger thought every girl heading to college should know how to fire a handgun. I put her off for two months. Then I got mugged and decided she had a point. Now can I ask you something? Or—no, I'll rephrase. Will you answer a question for me?"

He walked behind her down a surprisingly homey corridor. "I might."

She aimed a humorous look over her shoulder. "You said for every Jessie-Lynn there were fifty normal people in Blue Ridge. My question is, when do I meet one of the fifty?"

THE DRIVE THAT had taken Sig Rayburn two days going took him less than thirteen hours on the return trip. Fueled on bad coffee and hoarse from two and a half packs of cigarettes, he called his captain as he crossed the bridge into the city.

Ten minutes and a great deal of cursing later, the clearly out-of-sorts captain told him to report to his office at 9:00 a.m. and disconnected sharply.

Sig felt the sting but didn't care. Sera would be safe in Blue Ridge. Logan would see to that. He'd done the only thing he could, the right thing, he was sure. All he could do now was wait and hope her memory would return.

Unlike Wyoming, it was misty and cool in San Francisco. Fog slunk around the piers and the lower half of the city. He had time to grab breakfast, thirty minutes of sleep and a hot shower. By eight-forty he was back in the alley where he'd parked his car. He gave the dented roof a pat and the door a kick to open it.

A man in a black hoodie plodded past, drinking from a bottle in a bag. Sig spared him an uninterested look, then sighed at the interior of his Ford. He'd be swimming in trash soon.

He heard the sound behind him as he started to slide in. The blow to the side of his head stunned him—almost as much as the sight of the man who'd delivered it.

"You," he managed to croak.

Grinning nastily, the man stuck a gun in his throat. "No bandanna for you, cop." He shoved the tip in deep. "I'm saving it for the shrink." His face floated closer. "You're gonna tell me where she is."

"Go to hell," Sig managed to gurgle. "She's safe, and she will remember."

"Oh, I'm sure of it. What she won't do is live to testify."

"I'm not telling you squat."

"Not verbally," the man agreed. His gun made a quiet popping sound as the bullet discharged into Sig's throat. "But there are other ways, my friend." He folded his latest victim's body into the car, located his wallet and eyed the trash on the seat and floor. "Plenty of other ways."

Chapter Four

Sera could have slept for twenty-four hours. The twelve she got ended with a rough shake from Flo.

"Chief has to go to Casper for a meeting. You need to get up."

She stuffed Sera's clothes into a laundry bag, then picked up and examined her broken shoes.

"I can wear heels like this, but not Babe. She can hardly…"

"Walk some days. Got that, Flo." Sera fought off the effects of her latest nightmare. She was sliding from the surprisingly comfortable bed when the stack of suitcases caught her eye. "You unpacked for me?"

"I don't like ironing. What kind of doctor are you if you don't do feet?"

"I can do feet." In her dove-gray drawstring pants and white tank, Sera bent to look out the partly shaded window. "Will it be hot again today?"

"It's July, isn't it?" Flo dangled the strappy shoes. "You want me to see about getting these fixed?"

"Thank you." Biting back a smile, Sera offered the expected trade. "Would you like me to look at your sister's foot?"

"She'd appreciate that. But you tell Logan it was your idea. He said I wasn't to pester you."

"I will."

Cinching the canvas bag, Flo started for the door. "Logan'll be by in forty minutes. I've got flapjacks and blueberry syrup in the kitchen. Coffee too." She paused on the threshold. "When?"

Rocking the tension from her neck, Sera headed for the bathroom. "If you're talking about Babe, I can examine her when I get back from Casper, where I'm apparently going whether I like it or not."

Flo gave a satisfied nod. "Do your whatevers fast, and I'll feed you. Otherwise you're at Logan's mercy, and potato chips make a fine meal to him."

"It's a miracle cops live to retire."

"That last word's not one we use much in these parts, Doctor."

Why wasn't she surprised? Sera mused.

Still wondering where the normal people lived, she went into the bathroom to shower away her latest dream image—that of the Blue Ridge police chief's enigmatic face.

"DON'T LET HER out of your sight, Fred." Logan handed Sera a white hat with a braided black band, trapped her jaw and stared straight at her.

"No guns, no clever tricks, no tricky questions. Agreed?"

She pulled free and smiled. "You have a very low opinion of me, Chief."

"Must be the city cop coming out. I mean it, Sera."

"Yes, I know. Go on." She tried the hat for size and was pleased to discover it fit. "I won't ditch your dispatcher."

"Dispatcher slash senior deputy," the man called Fred corrected. He gave his boss two thumbs up. "Don't you worry, Logan. Me and the pretty doc'll get on just fine till your meeting's done."

Sera turned to examine the window of a small shoe store. Why couldn't the chief be more like his deputy? Huge, bald and in his late fifties, with a bull neck, a big belly and a smile as wide as the Platte River.

"You wanna walk, talk or shop, Doc?"

Fred's question brought a teasing smile.

"You're okay walking the streets of the county seat in the company of a marked woman?"

"No killer with half a brain's gonna shoot up a busy street at midday, Doctor—sorry, Serafina. That's a pretty name, by the way. Mean anything special?"

The sun glinted off the roof of a white delivery van. Sera popped her sunglasses on. "It means my mother had high hopes for my future. Didn't happen. I like Sera now."

He regarded her from under his own hat. "You and your ma at odds then?"

"Fifteen years worth and counting. There's no middle ground for us," she added before he could press. "We didn't see eye to eye on my future, so now we don't see each other at all."

"That's a shame, and I can say that because Flo and me have a girl, maybe six years up on you. We see her, but every time we do, it's either behind glass or on our doorstep in the middle of the night. She's an addict. Addiction's made her a thief. Thieving's sent her to jail four times. Guess we shouldn't throw stones considering our past, but we straightened out. I'm starting to think she never will. She owes money now, so I'm hoping against hope she won't show up at Logan's place. We live there, you know."

"With Logan? No, I didn't know. Or maybe I just didn't think. It's a big house."

"Came with…"

"The job, I heard." Hooking his arm, she asked, "Where does your daughter live, Fred?"

He snorted out a laugh. "Wherever the wind blows her. Like her ma and me that way. But you got your own problems, Doc. You don't need ours heaped on top of them. Word is you've got someone after you, someone who likes to kill. Any thoughts on why a person would do that over and over again?"

"A few, but nothing that really works. Whoa…" Raising her sunglasses, she ogled a purse dangling near a shop entrance. "That is one über cool bag. Bet it costs a fortune." She slipped around him and inside to flip the price tag. "Oh, yeah, fortune. Fourteen-ninety-five."

"That doesn't sound…"

"Fourteen hundred, Fred."

When he gaped, she caught his shirt and drew him back out. "Breathe deeply. The feeling will subside."

"Fourteen—fifteen hundred dollars? For a purse?"

"Well, it's leather." She glanced past him. "Dolce and Gabbana."

"But that's…"

"I know." Aware of the sun's increasingly strong rays, she steered him toward an outdoor café. "Do you like iced latte?"

"What?"

She grinned, then tugged on his shirt. "Coffee, cold, yummy. We can sit. You can tell me how you wound up in Blue Ridge and what it's like to work for Logan."

Fred ran a hand over his face. "Logan, right… Well, it's good. Best straight job I've ever had.

You probably know that Flo and me have done some shady things."

"We all have a past, Fred. The present matters more, don't you…think?" The last word emerged on a frown as a picture suddenly streaked through her head. Swinging away from the street, she pressed her fingers to her temples, trying to recapture it. "No, don't hide. Let me see you."

Fred came up behind her. "Are you okay? You want me to get Logan?"

Ignoring him for the moment, Sera struggled with the hazy image.

"Music," she said at last and, pivoting, searched for the source. "There was music playing in the background the night Andi died." She closed her eyes. "There's something behind it."

Fred sidestepped. "I'll get Logan."

"I need to hear it again." When he started off, she trapped his arm. "I'm good, Fred, really. I just need the music back. I saw something for a second. A hand, I think. And some kind of motion." She zeroed in on a muddy four by four truck. "That might be where it came from."

"You sure it was music, Doc, and not what you were saying?"

She started for the truck. "What were we talking about, do you remember?"

"Coffee, wasn't it? Or purses."

She cut across the street, skirted a group of people waiting to board a Greyhound bus and wound up back at the sheriff's office, where the truck was parked.

The cab of the vehicle was empty, but she made a slow circle around the hood.

Fred caught up and mopped his face with a red bandanna. "It's awfully hot, Doc. We could go inside, sit for a minute, see if we can find… Logan!" Relief colored his tone. "Am I happy to see you."

"I forgot a file. What are you doing?"

"Recreating," Sera said over her shoulder. She wanted to look at him, but that would destroy any chance she had of resurrecting the memory.

"Maybe we should…" Logan must have silenced Fred because he trailed off.

Sera continued to circle. "I saw a man's hand and part of an arm. He was wearing a watch with a chrome band. It was scratched and corroded in spots."

"Not a Rolex then," Logan said from the front of the truck.

"Tell him about the music," Fred suggested.

"I heard a song, or part of one, as this—I think this—truck drove past us." She bit her inner lip, drummed the box. "Might've been Bob Marley."

"'One Love'?"

"Maybe." But the title didn't trigger anything more. She made a flitting motion. "Sorry, it's gone. There was a watch, though, and it wasn't high end." She rubbed her wrist. "I saw a glove, too, but that's a given."

This time when Logan spoke, he did so from directly behind her. "What color was the glove?"

Her heart gave several hard thumps, which she controlled before turning. "Black. His fist was clenched, and it was striking something. A hard surface, possibly my desk."

"So this striking happened in your office."

Sera's head began to throb, but she pushed through it. "My office door was open. Andrea was in Reception when the security guard found her. I hit my head on my own desk, so I must have run in there." Leaning back against the side of the truck, she waved her hat in front of her face. "Sorry again, Logan, but that's all there is."

"It's more than you had before."

"Must be the mountain air."

She was doing it, she realized suddenly. Looking at him. Getting sidetracked. A baby step away from fantasizing about what it would be like to have that incredibly sexy mouth of his on hers.

Pushing off, she said, "Okay, that's it. Sun's frying my mind *and* my skin."

"Do you want to come inside?" he asked. "Meeting shouldn't take more than an hour."

Then he pulled a ringing cell phone from his waistband. "Logan," he answered with a trace of impatience.

Easing away, Sera searched her shoulder bag for the sunscreen she'd bought during one of Sig's filling station stops.

Logan's quiet, "When?" brought her head up and Fred away from his inspection of the four by four's front tires.

"Where?"

"Oh, hell." Her fingers stilled as a feeling of dread crept in.

"I'll get back to you, Captain." Logan broke the connection.

"He's dead, isn't he?" She said it simply and without inflection. But it hurt. It cut deep and it bled.

Fred looked from one to the other. "Who's dead? Someone in Blue Ridge?"

"His name was Sig Rayburn," Sera revealed. "He brought me here. He was a good cop with good instincts, but instead of being shot in the leg, this time he's dead."

Logan's eyes were steady on hers. "It's not your fault, Sera."

"Not directly," she agreed. "But indirectly— well, you decide." Removing her hand from her shoulder bag, she opened it. "I have his lucky rock."

HE'D DIED IN an alley. Like his partner, there'd been no bandanna, but every cop worthy of his badge knew who'd pulled the trigger.

That made it personal, Logan thought. Now, not only was he going to keep Sera safe, but he was also going to get the bastard who'd killed Sig and make damn sure he never saw the light of day again.

With his mallet, he drove a fence post deep into the ground, then gave the baling wire he'd been stringing a yank and secured it to the top.

He'd come to Blue Ridge to get away from this kind of crap—the gang leaders cops could never manage to touch, the targeted shootings, the senseless murders, all the garbage and destruction city life had to offer.

He'd been born and raised in a small town. He was where he wanted to be, doing what he wanted to do. And he still couldn't escape the urban nightmare.

He took a swing at another post and felt the impact race along his arms to his shoulders. He wouldn't let Sig or Sera down. But damn the woman, she was getting to a part of him he'd half forgotten existed.

Yes, she was beautiful. So were plenty of other females in the world. Surface meant nothing—he'd learned that lesson early on. And hormones tended to get in the way of good judgment.

Another slam, another shoulder-numbing jolt. It was after 7:00 p.m. According to the medical examiner, Sig had died around 8:30 a.m. He'd taken a single bullet to the throat, preceded by a sharp blow to the left side of his skull.

Fixing the last length of wire, Logan swiped

an arm across his forehead. He knew she was behind him before he turned. She smelled like jasmine and late summer roses. She was every man's gypsy fantasy.

Except for the sea-green eyes. Those were pure, storybook siren.

Without looking, he took a final pull from his Bud. "I'm not feeling chatty right now, Sera."

"I didn't think you would be." Coming around him, she dangled a half-done bottle of bourbon with an overturned shot glass on the top. "My uncle does trauma clinics on Sunday nights. He says sometimes we need a little poison to kick-start a difficult emotional process."

Logan drew his work gloves off with his teeth. "Sounds more like something you'd say."

"I just did." She glanced away. "Logan, I'm really sorry about Sig. I teased him a little—actually, a lot—for being superstitious. Now he's gone, and I have his rock, and who knows, it's a big universe, maybe there was something to his belief."

"Uh-huh."

Although her lips turned up, her eyes remained on the trees. "Figured you'd say that. But whether I believe in Sedona rocks or not, Sig did, and that's the point. What I don't understand is why he left town without it."

Logan downed the bourbon in a single swallow. When his throat reopened, he poured another. "Did he give it to you?"

"Only to hold."

"If he didn't ask for it back, he wanted you to have it."

"I was afraid you'd say that."

The ghost of a grin appeared as the liquor worked its magic. "Seems we're a step ahead of each other tonight." He handed her the glass. "To Sig," he toasted and raised the bottle to his lips.

Her eyes glinted before she tossed the liquor back. It amazed him that she only gasped once. "Med school," she explained at his prolonged look. "Real ass of an anatomy professor. His students, Andi and I among them, plotted his dissection at a dozen off-campus bars." Moving closer, she used her index finger to tip his hat back. "I'll be honest with you, Logan. You scare the hell out of me, and that's a big admission for me to make because I of all people know how to deflect this kind of fear."

"Yeah?" Capping the bottle, he set it and the glass on the post beside him. "So what say we do this now, and get it out of our systems."

It might have been surprise that flitted through her eyes. Whatever it was, the gleam behind it chased it out. She almost jerked when he caught her jaw in a light V. But then she relaxed and went with it—as he drew her closer and crushed his mouth to hers.

Chapter Five

Sera's mind blanked out. Her blood fired as need spiked. He tasted like bourbon-flavored sex.

Logan took his time, exploring her mouth with lazy thoroughness. It wasn't what she expected. Heat seared the edges of her control, but he didn't rush her, didn't take her on a wild ride to nowhere. Instead, he let the anticipation rise, made the hunger build. She might even have taken a hungry bite back.

Somewhat dizzy but decidedly intrigued, Sera gave his lower lip a tug, then reluctantly made herself end it.

His left hand dropped and his lashes lowered,

but he didn't step away. "Not the best idea I've ever had," he murmured.

"Not the worst either." A smile sparked her eyes. "But maybe not the smartest, all things considered."

"It's one of my bigger failings." With his fingers still wrapped around her neck, he stared down at her. "Sometimes I forget to consider the consequences of my actions."

Was any part of her body not tingling? Sera touched her thumb to each fingertip. "On the upside, Logan, that was some action you undertook. On the down, you're dredging up feelings I'm not sure I want to deal with. You're also undermining my resolve."

"Which is?"

"Present nightmare excluded, to control my own destiny."

"So there'll be no using the Force on you." The faint smile lingered as he unhooked his ringing cell phone. "Yeah, Logan."

Sera experienced a moment of regret when he

moved away, then reminded herself that distance was good. Another shot of bourbon wouldn't hurt either, but giving in would be weak, and she had no intention of becoming—well, a weak person.

"You sure your grandsons didn't take them?" Safely out of range, Logan threw his mallet in a Dodge truck that had seen better days and tossed Sera a set of keys. "Okay, I'll come by tomorrow. Meantime, check the barn and whatever other outbuildings are still standing."

When he bent to retrieve his work gloves, Sera tried not to notice how good he looked in his jeans and red T. "Is Grandpa Bulley missing some knives?" she asked.

A roll of baling wire joined the mallet. "Old Edgar locked up his sharpest knives years ago. He can't find his father's Winchester rifle. He's also minus a box of bullets and some food from his pantry—cooking spray, candy bars, chips, Twinkies."

"All the basics."

"To the non-medical types among us." He glanced down, arched a brow. "Did you walk all the way out here in those?"

"Oh, I can hike up any San Francisco hill in heels, but I'll be honest and admit that Fred drove me most of the way. I only had to make it in from the road." Her humor faded. "He's going to show up, isn't he, sooner or later?"

"Probably." Logan added his work gloves to the pile of tools and supplies. "Sig wouldn't have talked, but that never stops a serial killer. They find a way."

"Well, I feel better."

"You're a shrink, Sera. You don't need lies."

"No, but I wouldn't mind…" She stopped as a thought suddenly struck. "Dixon Dane! You—I—whoa." She spread her fingers. "I knew I'd seen you before. Did you know when Sig called—no, scratch that, you'd have known, because, although I don't believe in lucky rocks, a cop's memory, especially a pissed-off cop's, is pretty much infallible."

Logan scooped a second set of keys from the back bumper. "Dane killed a stranger on a train. Hacked a guy's head off with an ax he'd been carrying in his backpack."

"And that says sane individual to you?"

"It says he murdered an innocent man."

"He didn't fake us out, Logan. The voices directing Dane's actions make your Jessie-Lynn's aliens read like a ship full of Morks."

"He'll be on the street in seven years."

"Not based on my recommendation, he won't." But her right palm beat a restless tattoo on the leg of her jeans. "You're right, though, he will. And even if he's deemed fit to rejoin society, it won't erase what he's done." She sent him an assessing look. "That's why you're in Blue Ridge, isn't it, and not where you were?"

He shrugged. "New York, Boston, L.A., there was no difference in the end. Names, faces, coworkers. The crimes repeated, and time served became a joke. You want to drive?" He indicated the key ring in her hand. "Those are for you to use in case I'm otherwise occupied."

"Thanks." She exchanged the keys for the rock in the pocket of her jeans. "I know Sig gave it to me, but you were close to him so I figured you might…" She broke off at his expression. "What's that? Am I getting a look?" Dipping down, she peered under his hat. "Are you annoyed with me for offering to give you Sig's rock?"

"No. I'm not annoyed, and there's no look." Logan slammed the rear door of the truck. "I appreciate the gesture, but he wanted you to have it, not me."

"Yes, but…"

Reaching out, he closed her fingers around the smooth red rock. "Keep it until we nail the Blindfold Killer. You can give it to me then."

Heat speared up her arm, but she didn't react. "He told me it came from Sedona. But you already knew that, didn't you?"

"Yeah, I knew." He opened the driver's side door. "Choice of seats is yours, Doc."

She considered, then slid behind the wheel. "He said his nephew gave it to him."

"Yes."

"Look, I know you don't like answering…"

"I said yes, Sera." Before he slammed the door, he set his mouth on hers in a kiss that sent a streak of desire straight to her lower limbs and most of her thoughts into a black hole.

Most but not all, she realized as his answer suddenly registered.

Sig Rayburn hadn't merely been Logan's friend. He'd been his uncle.

BABE WAS LIMPING around the kitchen when she returned to the house. With a cryptic smile, Logan disappeared into the barn, leaving Sera to face Flo and her older sister alone.

Two hours and a long physical examination later, Sera had the woman booked for an X-ray at the hospital in Casper. Flo waited until Babe was seated in Fred's truck for the trip home before giving the tabletop an accusing jab.

"What were the words you used, and why did Doc Prichard say milk would make the problem go away?"

Sera went to the sink to wash her hands. "The term was plantar fasciitis. It refers to the long ligament on the bottom of the foot. As for the milk thing, no idea, unless it had to do with milk as a source of calcium."

Flo sniffed. "Man's a jackass."

"It's been mentioned. In any case, an X-ray will pinpoint Babe's problem, at which point it can be treated."

"By you."

"Well, I'm not really…"

"You're a doctor, aren't you? Have to be one before you can get into the head shrink stuff. I didn't fry all my brain cells when I was young."

"That's not exactly the point, Flo."

"You don't want to get involved."

Closer, Sera thought. "I'm not staying," she said, searching under the sink for a towel.

Flo whipped a fresh one out of the drawer. "S'pose I can't blame you for that. Our girl, Autumn, couldn't wait to get out… Should I go to Casper with Babe and Fred?"

"It's up to you. X-rays are a simple-enough procedure. Driving in hundred-degree heat, that's a killer."

Hanging the towel on a peg, Sera regarded the spoked wall clock. 10:15. Logic said she should be tired, but of course her mind kept drifting toward the barn.

"If you're going out, take the dog," Flo told her. "Chief's orders. You don't go anywhere alone." She snapped the light off, plunging the kitchen into the kind of darkness Sera seldom experienced in the city. "Stars'll help, but there's a flashlight in the mudroom if you need it."

Sera knew better than to take the woman's cranky tone personally. Still, she'd have thought someone called Moon Flower would have been a bit less prickly.

At her side, the dog gave a low growl.

"I know how you feel," she murmured.

And opening the door, she walked into a human wall.

It wasn't Logan—she knew that right away. This person kicked and flailed so erratically that a fist clipped her cheek and sent her stumbling into the jamb.

Ella barked, then leaped. At least, Sera thought she did. The room was so dark, she only caught glimpses of movement.

She heard shoes scraping on the floor as the intruder scrambled to avoid Ella's teeth.

Was it a woman? Didn't matter, she decided and grabbed the coat that billowed out in the person's wake.

"Let go, bitch," a raspy female voice snarled.

Sick of being jerked around by strangers, Sera hauled her sideways until she collided with the wall.

Or was it something else?

A light flared. "Are you hurt?" Logan demanded above the curses coming from the woman he was currently holding by the shoulders.

"No, but I can't say I think much of your visitors."

Twisting her head, the woman swore, first at her, then at Logan.

"Inventive," Sera remarked. "And I'm going to guess high as well." Letting her fingers fall from her bruised cheek, she summoned an unruffled smile. "You must be Autumn."

FLO'S DAUGHTER, A pixyish woman with handshorn hair and a wad of chewing gum in her mouth, vented her anger for a full minute until her mother appeared, apologized stiffly and marched her upstairs.

That left Sera alone with Logan, Ella and a sky full of stars.

"You don't get backdrops like this in San

Francisco," she remarked as they picked their way over the rocks and scrub toward the barn. "I can almost believe that's the whole Milky Way up there."

"Half of it anyway," Logan agreed. "Stars are different in the southern hemisphere."

She glanced over. "Have you been?"

"Twice. You?"

"Only to Brazil for a pag... To Rio, actually, when I was seven."

"You were eight, Sera, and you got the crown. Your friend Andrea was second runner-up."

The band that tightened around her midsection was instinctive. And unwarranted at this point in her life. She avoided a string of thorny weeds. "Do I want to know how you learned about that?"

"Probably not."

Okay, now the tightness was warranted. She snared his arm. "Tell me you didn't talk to my mother."

"Sig's personal calls are being forwarded

to my cell phone. He must have given her his number."

"Great. So now I have to suck it up and simmer, or let temper win and punch you."

Grinning, he helped her down a set of natural stone steps. "I'm flexible."

"My mother isn't. Was she drunk?"

"Maybe."

"Did she call me an ungrateful, self-centered bitch?"

"No comment."

"Bet she said I left her penniless, too, huh? Bled her dry, then let my uncle Jeffrey con me into coming to live with him."

"You know the woman, I'll give you that."

She wouldn't go for his throat, Sera promised herself. She'd deal, then she'd lock it away because it didn't matter any more. It couldn't matter—it could only hurt.

Her gaze touched on Orion's belt. "I was one of those kids, you know? With one of those mothers."

"Stage mother."

"That's the one. The beauty queen wannabe— her dream, not mine. I didn't 'wannabe' anything except normal."

"What happened?"

"Nothing I could control at first. Then later, nothing I could really object to. The prize money worked for both of us for a while."

"And after a while?"

Her smile had a sharp edge. "I didn't win. Fourteen years old, and I came in second at a tri-state pageant."

"Were you upset?"

"Not as much as my mom was. Does the word 'tantrum' bring any visuals to mind? On the surface, I got through it, but I was having a huge freak-out inside. Then I saw Andrea. We'd met at a pageant when we were five. At this particular event, I found her backstage, acting out every horrible thing I was feeling. She came fifth that night, probably because of a black eye she couldn't cover up. I remember thinking, well, yuck. Then I had an epiphany. I hated that world. I wanted to go to school like everyone else."

"Seriously?"

A portion of her tension dissolved at his tone. "Not a fan of the classroom, huh? Lucky for me, my mother's brother is a very grounded eccentric. He swooped in when my mother flipped out, said we needed some time apart and took me to live with him in L.A. I walked from the glam life that summer. End of story. Let's move on."

Once again, all she could see was Logan's incredible mouth—a mouth that had been igniting all kinds of feelings in her less than three hours ago.

His fingers skimmed down her throat while his eyes scanned her face. "Sera…" he began.

Then swore and shoved her to the ground as gunfire exploded out of the darkness.

Chapter Six

"You didn't see anything?" Draped over the seat of the Explorer, Fred looked from Logan to Sera and back. "Or anyone?"

"No and no," Logan replied.

They were en route to town from the Bulley farm, where Sera had been forced to spend a very long ninety minutes listening to old Edgar complain about his gout, his bursitis and the arthritic pain he continued to suffer in the two fingers he'd lost to frostbite thirty years ago.

After that, she and Logan had driven halfway to Casper to pick up Babe and Fred, whose SUV had died on the side of the highway. By the time they arrived, Babe had developed a whole new batch of symptoms for her to diagnose.

At this rate, Sera figured they'd be lucky to reach town by sundown.

The sun was in fact sinking when Logan noticed an approaching motorcycle. "Get the radar gun, Fred. That bike's coming fast. You belted in?" he asked Sera.

She shot him an exasperated look. "I have the front half of your dog on my lap, Logan. You couldn't launch me through the windshield if you tried." She swiveled her head as the motorcycle flew past. "Okay, rocket on wheels."

"Hundred and ten miles an hour," Fred confirmed. "Guess that means lights and siren." Before sitting back, he tapped Sera's shoulder. "Why do I see a bruise on your cheek, Doc?"

"Bad night vision."

"You sure you didn't have a tussle with Autumn? Flo thinks you did."

"No tussle," she lied and held on as Logan swerved to avoid a rabbit. Braking behind the motorcycle, he shoved Ella's butt off his leg and climbed out.

Ahead of them, a man with long brown hair and a droopy mustache dismounted.

Fred snorted out a laugh. "Here we go. Big smile for the small-town cop. 'Honest, Officer, I didn't mean to speed. Bike got away from me while I was taking in the beautiful scenery.' He's wasting his breath with that soggy spiel. Logan snacks on guys like him."

Sera watched cop and rider square off. Fred was right. The more Logan said, the more agitated the other man became. All they were seeing at this point were teeth. "He wants to take a swing," she noted. "Or, hmm, maybe not. Cop's got muscle and height and a stance that's telling him to give it his best shot."

As she watched, the man gestured in several different directions. His jerky movements suggested a blend of nerves and anger, thinly veiled. Logan, she decided, was very good at this.

Tipping her head to one side, she asked, "How did he wind up here, Fred?"

"Luck mostly. Fate if you believe. Our last chief was one of those pickers. You know the kind. Step outside a shop to check the color of a tie—you're a shoplifter. Pop a button while you're walking—that's littering. We had him for five years, until the mayor got sick of everyone complaining and started looking for better."

"And that was Logan."

"Yup. He was driving through town one day, heading for Montana. Nadine got to chatting with him, found out he was a cop and ran straight to the phone. Mayor and three of the town council members beat Logan's dinner to the table. Next thing we knew, he was taking a tour of the station. Now, let's go back to last night. I need you to give me the lowdown in detail because you don't seem panicky enough for a person who got shot at twelve times. Someone fired that many bullets at me I'd be shaking for days."

"Oh, I'm shaking, Fred. I'm just afraid to let it show." But she did let her mind slide back and a chill skate along her spine.

"Logan and I were heading toward the barn. The guy must have been hiding at the edge of the woods. If he'd waited another thirty seconds, he'd have had a better shot, but lucky for me, he fired prematurely."

"Gun or rifle?"

"Logan says gun. The bullets are being tested today."

"Lotta stars out and a big old half moon. You didn't see anything at all?"

"Only leaves, branches and some kind of animal that startled me as much as I startled it. Logan shouted at me to stay down, then he took off with Ella, but by the time they reached the road, the shooter was gone, mixed in with a dozen or more trucks coming from Frank's Diner."

"Did Logan talk to any of the drivers? Never mind, stupid question. 'Course he did. And no one saw a thing because the more they said, the better the chance they'd get charged with a DUI. People," he added in disgust.

Sera returned her gaze to Logan, who was sending the scruffy biker on his way. She couldn't help wondering if there'd been a specific reason why he'd chosen to leave the city. Cops like him seldom traded pace for peace.

She watched him walk toward them in his jeans, black hat and, for today at least, the requisite blue cop shirt. At the door, he unhooked his cell, talked for a few moments, then slid inside and tossed the phone on the dash.

When Ella whined, he motioned to Fred. "She needs a tree."

"Her and me both. Come on, girl."

Something in Logan's tone had a knot of resistance forming in Sera's stomach. "That was the police lab in Casper, wasn't it?"

"Ballistics report's in." His shielded eyes met her wary ones. "The bullets fired last night came from the same gun that killed Sig."

THE MEETING WITH the mayor at Town Hall took more than an hour because, big surprise, the man was delighted to discover a competent doctor in their midst. So delighted that he dropped his pants and showed Sera the spot on his butt where a large insect had bitten him.

Logan had no idea what she prescribed. Close-up inspections of male body parts wasn't in his job description. He escaped the office and let Nadine's mother, who was the mayor's secretary, flirt with him for a while.

It was after six before he reached the station. Back in the cells, the Bulleys sniped at anyone who'd listen, although they saved their nastiest barbs for the young deputy who had the misfortune to be their second cousin.

Logan's other deputies ignored both the Bulleys and their boss and vied for a look at Sera, who'd been waylaid outside the hardware store by a pregnant woman in curlers.

Perched on the dispatcher's desk, with a good view out the station window, Logan kept an eye on the sidewalk while he skimmed the file he'd been piecing together since yesterday.

Front and center was the ballistics report from last night's—whatever the hell it had been. Not a particularly adept murder attempt, that much was certain.

The killer had unloaded a dozen bullets from a nine-millimeter automatic, missed on all twelve counts, then backtracked at warp speed to his vehicle, where he'd successfully melted into the traffic on Boulder Road.

He hadn't laid down any rubber that Logan could see, and no one he'd questioned had noticed anything unusual.

Not that that surprised him. Workers heading back to camp from Frank's might notice a naked woman on the road, but one truck more or less, not a chance.

Okay, so the killer knew how to blend in. And he was a piss-poor shot when his gun wasn't pressed to a specific body part. What did that prove?

Not much in the grand scheme. But it did suggest he'd need to get close to kill again.

An unpleasant thought curled around the edges of Logan's mind. It had taken root early on, and he'd never quite managed to blow it off.

Sig had talked about a leak at headquarters, but what if that leak came with a twist? What if none of this was as it seemed?

Yeah, and what if he was jumping at old cop shadows?

Glancing up, Logan saw the pregnant woman drawing some kind of air picture for Sera.

"Chief?" Fred joined him with papers in each hand. "I got that playlist you wanted from the radio station in Casper. Bob Marley's there."

Setting his thoughts aside, Logan nodded. "Go for thirty minutes on each side and download the songs to an iPod. What else have you got?"

"Two full pages on our speeding biker. The name he gave you is real, but he's used others over the years."

"Arrests?"

"Three in Idaho, one in Colorado, two in Utah. He broke into a bank machine in Colorado and gave the cops stolen ID when he got picked up. Likeness on the driver's license was good though, and some time over the course of life's journey, he's had his fingerprints burned off, so it took them a while to sort things out. He's been living the free life for more than a year now, but—and here's the kicker—both the Colorado and Utah cops figure most of his crimes are someone else's brainchild. No idea whose, and he denies it all the way, but there you go. What kind of line did he give you?"

Logan read on. "He said his bike had been acting up, and he thought if he gave it a good, hard run, the problem would solve itself."

"Think he'll pay the fine or hightail it?"

"He hired on yesterday out at the resort. Says he's a roofer. He's put in eight hours so far."

"Might be worth losing the pay in order to finger you."

"I don't see it, Fred." Logan took another look

at Sera. "The guy had five bucks and a driver's license in his wallet, nothing but dirty laundry in his saddle bags and nerves stretched so tight I could've blown and watched them snap. He needs a fix. Either he knows someone here who can supply it, or he'll try his luck with our bank machines. Put Annabelle on night patrol with Biggs and Wendell, then call Johnny Abraham at the construction site and get him to send me a list of all the workers he's taken on since yesterday afternoon. Tell him I want that list updated every time he adds a new name. Same goes for anyone looking to hire here in town."

Fred cast a worried look at Sera. "You think whoever's after the doc will try to hide in a crowd of strangers?"

"It's possible. He's good with disguises. He might also camp out in the woods. Give Walter and Toby that detail. I want all the sites in the area investigated, and that includes the big one on Edgar Bulley's farm. Ditto the bed and breakfasts, the Lake's Inn and the Bear Hotel. I want details on anyone who matches the general description I gave you. Clear?"

Fred scratched an ear. "That's a tall order at this time of year, Logan. Tourists everywhere. Hunters, fishing folk, backpackers, bird watchers and, I think, a group of naturalists out near Sprout Lake. Not sure any of us will want to check them out."

Logan flipped to the next page in the file. "You never seen anyone naked before?"

A flush crept up Fred's thick neck. "Saw things that would make your hair turn during the Summer of Love, but it's a bit uncomfortable interrogating people who're letting it all hang. Hard to know where to put your eyes."

That wasn't Logan's problem at the moment. His eyes didn't want to leave Sera, no matter how many directives they received from his brain.

"Just ask the necessary questions, and look anywhere that works for you."

The big man didn't speak for a minute, but he

didn't leave either. When he shifted his weight for the fifth time, Logan gave up trying to ignore him. "Something else, Deputy?"

He cleared his throat. "About the doc. I was wondering…"

"I'm not going to tell you who's after her. You only need to know that someone is."

A windy sigh emerged. "I suppose that's fair. But twelve bullets? That's an awful big number. Whoever he is, he must want her pretty badly."

"He does."

The edgy feeling crawled through Logan's belly again. Something there, his instincts warned. Then his gaze rose to the window, and he felt a spike of fear shoot into his throat.

Sera was gone…

HE'D OBSESSED ABOUT her since it happened, reliving the scene again and again. Beat himself up over it.

He wanted to beat her instead.

He saw himself in his mind, prowling the

street outside the medical building, waiting, watching. The light on the fifth floor was on. She was working late.

Minutes turned to hours. Rain bounced off the roof of his car. Then, finally, the front door opened.

He recognized her red trench coat instantly.

Not yet, not yet, he cautioned himself. She was going to the all-night deli. She'd go back up. He'd get her then.

She emerged from the deli with a box and hugged the building walls so the rain wouldn't soak her. She used a key card on the door and went back inside.

He counted to ten, then used his own stolen key card and followed.

Child's play. Five flights of stairs, and he was there.

Do it quick. That was the best way.

He eased the office door open. She had her back to him. She was hanging her coat on a hook to dry.

He knew where the light switch was. He snapped it down. It wasn't completely dark, but who cared? Five strides brought him to her. He hooked an arm around her neck. Bye-bye, gorgeous.

One slash of his knife, and she was dead.

He let her drop. Done.

No wait. What was that sound?

An inner door opened.

"Andi, this patient's…" Green eyes locked on his.

He wanted to lunge, but shock turned his legs to lead.

It took forever to reach her. When he did, she kicked him in the nuts and ran.

A door slammed. He heard her on the phone. Pain screamed through his body, but he knew she couldn't get out, couldn't get past him. She was trapped.

He almost tripped over the dead body. He wanted to kick it aside. Wrong, it was all wrong.

He crashed through the door, breathing like a bull, shouting. Plan, what plan? Nothing left now but to fix it fast and get the hell out.

She'd called someone. His palms went clammy, but rage kept him going.

She was fast. He was faster—and still between her and the door.

He caught her. She fought. He went for his knife. She kicked him again. He shoved. She fell, hit her head, stopped moving.

"Dr. Hudson?"

He heard a voice on the other end of the phone.

Run, he ordered his lead-weighted legs. People would come. Use the fire escape. Get away and hide…

He called in sick the next day. Ear to the ground, though. He listened to the other "invisibles." They heard it all.

His mind leaped ahead.

Luck was with him. She couldn't identify her friend's killer. She didn't remember…

Alone for the moment, he looked up at the vast Wyoming sky, arms spread, face rapt.

Yes, Papa, there is a God!

Chapter Seven

"You're going to pull my arm out of the socket, Logan." Sera twisted on her wrist. "I'm not a criminal, and I'm not your dog. Stop playing caveman cop and let me go."

He did, but only, she suspected, because they'd reached the front door of the drugstore and couldn't go through it at the same time.

"Back to Town Hall," he said once they were outside.

"Not your dog," she reminded. Bending, she ruffled the retriever's ears. "No offense, Ella."

The dog barked and plopped down next to her

on the sidewalk. The dark sidewalk, she noted in surprise.

She felt Logan staring, then realized that more than a few people around them were doing the same thing and sighed.

"The woman's eight and a half months pregnant. She asked me what products she could safely use in order to sit for more than ten minutes at a time." Her temper pricked at his continued stare. Disinclined to smooth the edges, she retraced her steps and went toe to toe with him. "You're a cop, Logan, you protect people. I'm a doctor. I help those same people with medical conditions. Try not being able to sit in a chair, and see how you feel after six weeks. Oh, but first strap on a pregnancy suit. You won't be asking for help, pal—you'll be begging for it."

"You weren't in the drugstore the first time I looked."

"Yes, I was. You just didn't see me because the night clerk, who lives upstairs, was afraid that George, who's been losing weight steadily over the past six months, has stomach cancer."

"George is the clerk's dog," Logan said.

"Thank you, I discovered that. Unfortunately, he neglected to mention it until I'd gone up. What he did mention is that your Dr. Prichard dabbles in veterinary medicine. If I were you, I'd stick with the overworked but legitimate town vet. George has two teeth that need to be pulled and his diet consists mainly of kibble. Prichard didn't even look in his mouth. He felt his ribs, then pronounced that the dog had two months to live. As a tactless parting shot, he told the owner that Nadine's border collie is expecting a litter of puppies in August."

Catching her chin, Logan looked directly into her eyes. "Cell phone, Sera. You have one. Next time you decide to hold an impromptu clinic, use it."

"Love to." She moved her lips into a smile. "As long as, next time, you remember to clip yours on and not leave it on your dash." She widened her eyes. "I left a message, Logan. Twice."

He was swearing softly when a man with a prominent Adam's apple strolled past. "Evenin', Chief." He winked at Sera. "You tell him what's what, Doc. Just don't ride him so hard he leaves town."

"Keep walking, Harry," Logan suggested. His eyes were fixed on hers. "Town Hall, Dr. Hudson. Please."

Because far too many people were staring at this point, Sera located the large, wood-fronted building across from the drugstore and, with an unpromising look at Logan, started toward it.

The century-old structure had a wide, worn stoop, mullioned windows and a sign above the entrance that had apparently been nailed in place by someone too inebriated to see straight. The hinges on both doors screeched, the pine floors sagged in the middle, and the air smelled of stored apples and old books. She noticed that one of the side windows was broken. A green trash bag duct taped over the hole flapped open at the top, allowing both insects and the omnipresent wail of country music inside.

When the overhead lights blinked on, Sera spied a stack of wooden crates with the letters BRD painted on the sides directly ahead of her.

"Blue Ridge Days," Logan said without looking. "It's a mid-summer tradition. Means more money for local businesses and more work for me and my deputies." He snagged her arm before she could evade him. "You could have called the station."

She could also tell him off and leave the hall. But that would be foolish and ungrateful. He was only trying to keep her alive.

So she released a breath and gave the stack of chairs beside her a vexed nudge with her knee. "I'm not used to living like this, Logan, under scrutiny twenty-four hours a day. Do you really think the Blindfold Killer would follow me into a drugstore half a block from the police station?"

"He fired twelve shots at you in the police chief's backyard. Yeah, I think he'd follow you and take out anyone who got in his way."

"Oh, good. Now I don't just feel bad—I also feel guilty for endangering the lives of a thirty-something store clerk and a woman with child."

"Children. Prichard says she's having twins."

"Don't think so, Ace. She's not large enough. I felt her belly. That's one big baby she's carrying. No room inside for two."

"You sure, Doc? Twins run in her husband's family."

"They run in my mother's, too, but as you see, I'm an only one."

"Trust me, Sera, one's more than enough."

A round of cheers and catcalls reached them through the broken window. She hoisted herself onto a crate. "Sounds like stripper night at the Main Street saloon."

"You could say." Logan prowled a little. "Sometimes Ginny gets tanked and starts up a game of strip poker in the back room."

"Of her saloon?"

"Garage. She fixes vehicles—cars, trucks, motorcycles, strollers, anything that rolls. Her last name's Bulley."

"Of course it is. And she gets tanked on…?"

"Whatever's left in the barrels my deputies and I don't find and her cousins haven't sucked dry." A gleam in his eyes lightened the mood. "Wanna join the game?"

"FYI, Chief, I went to college. I've done more than…"

It came out of nowhere, a razor-thin beam that sliced through the wall in her mind and allowed a brief but vivid image to sneak out.

She focused her eyes downward and let her heel hit the side of the crate. "Okay," she said softly, "that was weird." Her gaze slid to the flapping trash bag. "I saw him—his watch, I think, and his coat, some kind of lightweight khaki." The bag flapped again as a breeze stirred the air. "I remember mothballs—and some other smell buried under it." She tried to separate the components. It wasn't men's cologne. She tapped the crates beneath her. "What's inside these?"

"Decorations. Streamers, bunting, signs."

"Stored in mothballs," she assumed. "Which must have been the trigger. It's gone back to blurry now. But I saw a khaki coat and the chrome watch again, so I know it's the same guy." She breathed out. "Damn, this is so frustrating." On more than one level, she reflected, hopping down.

When the hoots and catcalls reached them again, her lips curved into a slow smile. "Tell me, Chief, can anyone join Ginny Bulley's game?"

"Far as I know." His eyes dropped to her breasts, then rose with a glitter. "You're not wearing much in the way of clothing, Sera. Couple bad hands, you'll be down to your underwear."

"Lingerie," she corrected and, giving into temptation, ran a finger from his throat to his chest. "Black and lacy, the kind of feminine garments men are terrified to buy."

"You think?"

"Probably not as clearly as I should, but what if we do this." She took a suggestive step closer, flicked a finger between them. "A one-on-one contest, you and me, beyond the parameters of the usual game. I win, you buy me dinner. You also agree to cut me some slack when I'm in a relatively safe place. You win, I buy, and I'll accept your twenty-four-seven surveillance rules without a fuss."

The glitter became a gleam. Trapping her hand he brought it to his mouth and kissed her knuckles. "It's a deal, Doc. We'll leave Ella at the station. She's not as big a fan of black lingerie as I am."

She gave him a quick, teasing kiss. "You're counting chickens, pal. Never a wise move in my experience."

With a smile she knew she shouldn't trust, he swept a hand toward the door. "After you, Doc."

A feather-light shiver danced along her spine as another image suddenly appeared. Not of a man wearing khaki and chrome, but of the man behind her wearing nothing at all.

"YOU CHEATED."

Sera preceded Logan into Tommy Gray Wolf's bar. She wore his hat, his cop jacket and all of her own clothes.

Kenny Chesney poured from four speakers mounted high in the dusty rafters. It was the barman's ode to the present. Given a choice, Logan knew Tommy would play Johnny Cash from morning to night.

Setting his mouth next to her ear, he nodded forward. "Head for the back corner. The people there are leaving."

"How many bars does this town have?" she asked over the music.

"Nine or ten." He stopped a tourist from snatching the hat off Sera's head. "Depends on your definition and whether or not you include Frank's Diner."

"Or Ginny Bulley's back room." Halting, she pushed the hat from her face and sent him a wary stare. "Back to the cheating thing. I saw you do it. What I don't understand is why you stacked the cards so I'd win." Her gaze fell to the front of his jeans. "You like women's lingerie, right?"

"Do I need to answer that?"

She smiled and started walking. "No, and maybe I understand after all. Not necessary, though. I played poker in med school. I also have a patient who's a compulsive pretty-much-anything-you-can-name. He talks to me, but only if we play five-card stud during our sessions. Because gambling's the least of his problems, I took the deal. He's taught me how to cheat and spot a cheater. I'm helping him overcome his need to set fire to any structure bigger than a phone booth."

"You're joking."

"I never joke about patients, Logan. It might seem like a lighthearted approach to a serious problem, but it's working. In any case, he isn't the most dangerous arsonist I've taken on."

By the time they reached the table, Kenny had given way to George Strait. "Sounds like an interesting career, Doc." Logan pulled out a chair for her, scanning the crowded room for the third time in as many minutes. "Ever worked with a serial killer?"

"No, but I've collaborated on several murder cases—beyond our creepy common dominator. Logan." She touched his arm. "If he's here, he won't do anything. Suicide's not this guy's deal. Completing his specific agenda is."

"Sure of that, are you?"

"As sure as I can be with only slivers of information to go on."

"I wouldn't call that a reassuring assessment."

"That's because you're approaching this from the perspective of a cop who's thinking protection rather than motive." She leaned in to stage whisper, "He's not done. If suicide was his goal and Andrea had been his final victim, Sig and his partner would still be alive, I'd be home in bed and the Blindfold Killer would be in a body bag. My guess is he has more people to murder, or he wants to go on hiatus for a while. Either way, not done."

When Logan didn't respond, she nudged his arm with her shoulder. "Ground Control to Major Tom. You still with me, or is the BK's motive starting to interest you?"

He ran his gaze around the busy room. "Everything interests me, Sera, but motive's not relevant here—unless Paxton's suddenly decided that killing beautiful brunettes is the way to go."

The thought of her partner brought a twinge of regret. "Andi and I should have been better friends." She drew an absent crown on the table. "Her ancestry was Scottish. Mine's Irish. People used to call us the Celtic sisters. One of her patients who was into astrology insisted we had a

Gemini connection. She said we shouldn't work together because of it. Something about spatial displacement and overlapping dimensions. Bottom line, we should dissolve our partnership before all hell broke loose in our astrological spheres."

"Was this patient psychic?"

"No idea. She was definitely bipolar, which was Andi's main concern." Sera watched a man and woman unapologetically making out on the dance floor. "There's no professional connection between Andi and Hugh Paxton, Logan. The San Francisco police went over her life in detail. It has to be a personal link, if not to the first eleven, then somehow to his last three victims. Assuming there are any links involved."

Logan sat back. "You want my feeling, cop to shrink?"

She'd like a great deal more, actually, but truth had its place and this wasn't it. "Love it," she said. "Are we talking random or calculated here?"

"Calculated. Likely convoluted. Definitely personal in terms of each victim."

"So, pretty much textbook then. Some wrong being made right in Paxton's eyes."

"The investigational stumbling block being that said wrongs often seem perfectly right to a serial killer."

"Whose values are dictated by his emotional barometer, which in turn frequently harkens back to some childhood dysfunction either unnoticed or induced by the mentors and or peers... Blah, blah."

Logan chuckled. "Tired, are you?"

"And hungry."

As if cued, the drinks and appetizers they'd ordered at the door appeared on the table courtesy of a harried server. She had a cigarette tucked behind one ear and a cloth wrapped around her left hand.

"It's nothing," she said at Sera's raised brows. "Fire in a frying pan. Tommy doused it." She rapped Logan's shoulder. "Abe's at the bar, says you want to talk to him. I'm due for a break. I'll sit with the doc, keep your seat warm."

Almost as good a bodyguard as Fred, Logan reflected. "Back in ten," he told Sera and was glad to finally see an amused expression.

Johnny Abraham, called simply Abe, owned seven plaid shirts, one beer buckle belt and a nineteen-fifties truck that only ran because Ginny Bulley was the best mechanic in Wyoming. He'd been hiring steadily since early spring and subcontracting for the last three months.

When he spotted Logan, he gave the man beside him a shove. "Find another seat, Mel."

"I'm Travis."

"Well, you smell like Mel. Go on, get. Chief wants a word."

"Yeah? Well, I've got a beaut of a word for you, Chief." The beer-bellied worker tapped the side of his nose. "It's Bulley—as in watch out for the ones who aren't behind bars. Heard rumblings about the two oldest." At his boss's glare, Travis shrugged and left.

"Man's got the brains of a billy goat, but he's strong as an ox." A trio of chins wobbled beneath Abe's fully dentured smile. "What's on your mind, Logan? Besides that pretty doc you've been showing the sights to these past few days?"

Because he'd left his mug on the table, Logan went with a glass of beer and another scan of the room. "I want names, Abe."

"I know." He dug in the pocket of his shirt. "Only have three, and all of 'em came with references."

Logan took the folded paper. "You check any of those references out?"

"Yeah right, I got oodles of friggin' time to do that. I'm only a month behind schedule, and old gloom and doom Joe's predicting two feet of snow by Halloween. Hell, Logan, I'd hire Edgar Bulley if he came looking." Raising his beer, Abe squinted at the door. "Speaking of... Unless

I need my glasses more than Travis thinks I do, two of old Edgar's dumbass grandsons just lumbered in. Could be they're looking for you."

"Looking for trouble anyway." Although he didn't expect it would amount to anything—the killer, a known suspect, wouldn't be likely to hire on to work in plain sight—Logan pocketed the list and kept his eye on the glowering men.

Swiveling back to the bar, Abe bumped his elbow. "She staying?"

"No."

"Why not?"

Because complication, strong emotions and lust were things he didn't want or need in his life. Because she was a psychiatrist and he was a cop, and those two professions, as proved by the Dixon Dane case, didn't mix. And because he'd been doing just fine without her.

She wasn't his type, and no way in hell was he hers. The big city burnout that had landed him here hadn't done its phoenix-rising-from-the-ashes thing yet. He was no bargain for any woman at this point, let alone a dark-haired, green-eyed siren whose job was to fix screwed-up people. To get inside messed-up minds.

To get under his damn skin…

Between that last thing and the growing twist of doubt in his belly, Logan's mood began to deteriorate. Raising his beer, he slid his gaze to the corner table.

And saw the biker he'd ticketed that afternoon skulking across the floor toward Sera.

Chapter Eight

"You cook, you get burned." The server, whose name was Jenny-Lynn, shrugged. "It's no big thing."

"Bet it stings." Sera rewrapped her hand and tore the ends of the towel to tie it. "I can write you a prescription to manage the worst of the pain."

"I wouldn't say no." Jenny-Lynn gave her fingers a casual flex. "You got something going with our chief of police?"

Mostly in her head, Sera thought, but shuffled the fantasy aside and went with Logan's story. "Actually, I'm on vacation. Logan's uncle told me about Blue Ridge Days, and I was free, so I figured why not explore the Big Horn Mountains?"

"Uh-huh." The woman, a self-described hot mama with a no-nonsense attitude, fifty-plus years under her belt and cabernet-colored hair, picked up Logan's beer, studied the thin line of foam and took a deep swallow. "You heard about my sister yet?"

Sera tread carefully. "If her name's Jessie-Lynn, yes, I have."

"She's ten years younger than me and loony as a Warner Brothers' cartoon. She saw you for the first time today. Called me straight away, said that pretty-as-a-picture doc was gonna steal our police chief out from under us unless we did something big."

"Should I be worried?"

"Hard to say. Knowing Jess, she's talking alien intervention. Now me, I'm more inclined to talk practical, and I get a little oochey think-ing about this town without Logan. He keeps things running smooth, and, hon, you gotta know, the ladies love him, local and tourist."

"Fancy that." Leaning in, Sera let her eyes dance. "Police chief and tourist attraction rolled into one. That's some weighty twofer."

"You teasing me?"

She laughed. "Yes, I am. Look, would you and Jessie-Lynn feel better if I admitted that I'm really here because I had a stalker after me in San Francisco and the detective in charge of the case thought it would be a good idea for me to leave the city?"

Jenny-Lynn stopped a match halfway to her cigarette, shook it out and scooted her chair closer. "Honey-lamb, I am all ears. Do you think this stalker followed you to our little mountain town?"

"Maybe." Because her wine sucked, Sera took a sip of Logan's beer, and immediately wanted to spit it out. "That tastes like sewer."

"Lines need cleaning. We'll get to it when the regulars start griping."

Sera pushed the mug to the center of the table. "That's just plain gross, Jenny-Lynn."

"You think?" The server braved another large swallow. "Tell me, Doc, d'you know what this stalker of yours looks like, or are we talking stranger?"

Sera selected a red nacho from the plate. "Stranger, I think. I might have caught a glimpse of him once, but nothing definite. He wears a watch with a chrome band on his left— no wait—on his right wrist." She halted mid crunch. "How did I know that?" Then frowned. "How did I miss it?"

Jenny-Lynn struck a fresh match. "You're losing me, hon."

Sera's mind skipped back. The police report said the Blindfold Killer had slashed Andi's throat from behind with a left to right motion. With his right hand. Most right-handed people wore watches on their left wrists. Andi's killer hadn't.

She tapped a contemplative finger on the table. "Maybe he's ambidextrous."

"Still lost. Are we talking about your stalker?"

Sera zoned back in. "What? Oh, no. I was thinking about a patient."

"I heard you helped Babe and the mayor. And Nadine's cousin who's having twins she and her husband can't afford."

"I suppose I did, but…"

"You don't call them patients?"

"I was only trying to…"

"Sure, more people than you might like know your business, but those same people are also there when and if you need them."

"Look, I like it here. It's just…"

"Dr. Prichard is a complete jackass. Unfortunately, he's all we've got. Doc Faldo and his wife Doc Faldo retired last year and left town. Now a resort's coming in. We don't need one doctor, we need at least four, and for my money, Prichard can hightail it to some other state. Do you know anybody who'd be willing to help you out at the clinic?"

Sera regarded her with patience. "I'm not staying, Jenny-Lynn, and even if I was, technically I'm not a family physician. I'm a psychiatrist."

Jenny-Lynn hooked an arm around the back of her chair. "You got Babe to like you," she began, then rolled her eyes when the owner shouted from the bar. "Guess recess is over." She crushed out her cigarette. "Think before you decide," she said and was gone before Sera could respond.

She was sliding Logan's mug absently toward her when a man's fingers spread across the top.

"Hey there, sugar. Name's Wayne, and I got a powerful thirst building. D'you mind?" With his flat brown eyes on her face, the biker Logan had pulled over that afternoon removed the mug from Sera's unresisting fingers and raised it to his mouth.

"You must have a cast-iron stomach," she

remarked when he didn't flinch. "That beer's crap."

"Whole town's crap. Except for you. Sheriff's a complete…"

"Police chief," she interrupted. "Former homicide detective. If that matters to you."

"Why should it?" His chin jutted. "You think I can't handle a cop? Watch it, pal," he snarled. "That's my arm you're poking."

Across from Sera, a big man with Bulley features and hands the size of ham hocks gripped Wayne's shoulder and lifted him off his feet.

"Go away." He set his other hand on the knife in his belt. "I got business with the lady."

This couldn't be good. Sera stood—only to find herself staring into a second man's chest. Bulley number two, she presumed.

"You're not leaving us, are you, Doc?" Number Two's smile mirrored his brother's. "Cause we wanna get some things straight. Beat it," he snapped at the biker, whose mustache had begun to tremble.

"Leave him alone." Sera jerked back when the second Bulley reached for her.

A tanned arm wrapped around Number Two's throat, squeezing just hard enough to draw a chocking cough.

"Call her reaction a no and back off, Lloyd. You, too, Victor."

The Bulley named Victor tossed the biker aside as if he were made of cardboard. "We got a bone to pick with you, Logan."

"Figured you might."

"Her, too."

Sera sidestepped the finger he attempted to thrust in her face and glanced at his belt. "Uh, Logan…"

"I see it." Logan's flexed forearm turned the cough to a hiss. "For your brother's sake, you want to leave that knife where it is."

"Two of us and only one of you," the trapped Bulley growled. "Odds ain't exactly in your favor."

"No? Huh." Logan's elbow clipped Lloyd's jaw so swiftly that Sera missed the move.

The dazed man mowed the biker down, then staggered into a skinny man about to take a drink of beer. The beer flew, the biker landed on his butt and three pairs of hands made a grab for the fallen Bulley's shirt.

"Well, hell," Logan said on a breath.

It was the last really clear thing Sera heard. The flying beer seemed to galvanize half the males in the room and more than a few of the females.

A man in plaid with three chins and a frantic look on his face barreled into the fray. "Leave it be, Derek," he shouted.

"Put your glasses on, old man. I'm Travis."

"Behind the bar, Sera." Logan shoved her toward the pass-through where Jenny-Lynn was waving an arm.

"Come on, hon," she called. "Tommy's gonna hit the lights. That'll put a damper on things."

"Don't count on it." Sera did a double take as

the biker yanked a switchblade from his boot. A second later, someone stumbled into her shoulder. "Toby?" She helped Logan's junior deputy regain his balance. "Did your cousin just punch you?"

He swiped gamely at a bloodied lip. "They're a little riled tonight is all."

A little riled and a lot drunk, Sera reflected. Either their whiskey barrels were bigger than Logan realized or the Bulleys had another still up and running on their farm.

Jenny-Lynn continued to motion her forward. Music blared overhead. It was like a scene out of a B movie, except the blood here was real and there was no way to separate the good guys from the bad.

She'd almost reached the pass-through when the room went dark.

"Gotcha, Doc," Jenny-Lynn said.

She caught hold of Sera's jacket—a split second before Sera caught the smell of mothballs.

She started to swing around. "Jenny, where's Lo...?"

It was all she got out, and the last thing she remembered.

Something came down hard on her head. Like thick fog rolling in, deep shadows gave way to solid black, where noise, thought and music simply disappeared.

"LOGAN?" HIS YOUNG deputy sounded unsure.

Logan blocked a full-face punch and swung the drunk in front of him into an arm lock. "Toby, get to the bar and tell Jenny-Lynn to turn on the damn lights."

He had to toss the drunk he was holding aside so he could yank his junior deputy out of the way of Victor Bulley's fist. When the big man snarled and raised an arm, Logan went with the obvious and kicked him in the groin.

"Go," he ordered Toby.

"I won't make it," Toby protested, but at a

push from Logan, he endeavored to forge a path in the general direction of the bar.

Someone large and heavy slammed into his back. Logan spun, prepared—then blew out a breath when he realized it was Fred.

"What's going on?" the big man demanded. "I came in the door and almost got tackled by Lloyd Bulley."

Logan used his fist on a man who was lining Fred up from behind.

"How did you see him?" Fred demanded, peering at the floor.

"I worked a lot of night shifts in L.A." Logan shook out his bruised knuckles. "Follow Toby to the bar. I want the lights on—now."

A flashlight beamed wildly in front of him. "Logan!" Breathless and pointing, Jenny-Lynn clutched his wrist. "Someone took Sera."

"What?" Her statement cost him a hard shot to the ribs.

Ignoring the pain that screamed through his body, he gripped Jenny-Lynn's arms and propelled her backward. "What happened? What did you see?"

"The room was dark, so not much. I had my hand on her sleeve, then I didn't." She gripped him back. "I don't know how I know it, but I felt someone hit her. Air moving maybe. And I heard her say something about mothballs."

"Could you tell which direction they went?"

"No, but I'd guess one of the side doors. Back's too hard to get to through the kitchen, and you can forget the front."

"I'll go left," Fred volunteered and began plowing through the field of bodies.

Logan took her flashlight, used his forearm on someone's throat and deposited Jenny-Lynn at the pass-through. "Get those lights on and make sure both Bulleys are still here."

"I can hear Lloyd squawking, so he's here for sure." She dug stubby fingernails into his arm. "Find her, Logan, before…" A swallow ended the statement. Turning, she shouted the owner's name.

Logan followed the long bar to the second door. Could be a Bulley had grabbed Sera out of spite, but that was probably wishful thinking.

"Logan, I wanna…whoa, no, take it back."

Logan pointed the gun he'd drawn from his waistband at the ceiling and fixed his eyes on Victor Bulley's shadowed face. "Where's your brother?" he demanded.

A sneer appeared. "None of your f…"

An uppercut sent him sprawling over a table that cracked under his weight.

Logan had no idea what the killer's plan might be when operating on unfamiliar ground. The Bulleys would do anything short of murder if the price was right, and Sera's abductor could undoubtedly playact with the best of them. He might have paid a Bulley to take her.

He reached the exit and pushed through to the relative silence of the alley. A row of trucks lined one side, metal trashcans the other.

Toby rushed through the door behind him. "Fred just told me…"

"Go right," Logan ordered. "Check every vehicle."

He took the longer line on the left. He'd barely reached the first truck when an engine roared to life.

"Got you, bastard," Logan growled as light flooded the alley. Taking aim, he went for the tires.

The truck slammed into reverse. He shot twice. The man in the truck retaliated, letting five rounds go. Ramming the side of Abe's Hummer, he fired again, then jumped out and bolted into the night.

Logan heard Toby go down behind him and swore.

"I'm okay," Toby called weakly. "He winged my arm."

The truck's tires squealed. Logan smelled burning rubber. The box was wedged against Abe's heavy vehicle. Stones flew in all directions. Cutting through the twin beams, Logan raised an arm against the rock spray and yanked the driver's side door open.

He saw her in the back of the extended cab, facedown on the seat. Unmoving.

"Sera!" Kicking a stone off the gas pedal, he shoved the truck out of gear and reached for her.

Was she breathing? He pressed his fingers to the pulse point in her neck. Fast but steady. And there was no trace of red on the cracked seat.

Logan let his forehead drop onto her hair. She was alive.

And he was in deep, deep trouble.

Chapter Nine

"I don't have a concussion." Arms folded, Sera regarded the line one of his deputies had drawn on the station floor. "You don't seriously expect me to do this."

Logan sat back at his desk, hat forward, booted feet propped on top. "Walk the line, and the key to the clinic's yours. Otherwise it'll be up to Doc Prichard to deal with the fallout from last night's fisticuffs."

"It was a barroom brawl, and I happen to know you were in there brawling with the best of them. You also saved my life, so thank you.

Again." At his placid stare, she sighed. "Still have to navigate the line, huh?"

"Do it, and I can go out to the practice range, blow the guy away a few dozen times."

The killer had left a white bandanna, Sera recalled with a chill. He'd stuffed it under the seat of his truck, or rather a truck stolen from Edgar Bulley's barn.

There'd been no non-Bulley paraphernalia inside, and she didn't anticipate any better luck in terms of fingerprints. Besides, what would it prove if they did find one of Hugh Paxton's prints? Identifying him wasn't the key. Unmasking him was.

Resigned, Sera walked to the top of the line. "I'm only doing this once, Logan, so sit up and take notice."

He didn't, but she saw his lazy smile and knew he was watching. Closely.

Five seconds later, she pivoted ninety degrees in three-inch heels, then strolled toward him, palm out. "Mission accomplished, Chief. Where's the clinic?"

It took two minutes to get there from the station and less than half that time for Sera to understand what everyone had been telling her from the start about Rufus Prichard.

Chimpanzees could have done a better job of organizing and maintaining the town's limited medical equipment. The BP monitor had a torn cuff, the stethoscope was dirty and the scale fell apart when she touched it.

"You have paramedics, right?" She flicked through the filing cabinet and wasn't impressed.

"Four of them," Logan confirmed. "They take emergencies straight to Casper."

Sera looked around, considered. "Jenny-Lynn's right. You'll need more doctors when the resort's done. What about nurses?"

"Only one. She's sixty-six and married to Jenny-Lynn's uncle. She worked with Prichard for two days after she retired from her hospital job in Casper. On Tuesday afternoon, she marched across the street to inform me that she was putting an old Norse curse on him. So far it hasn't kicked in."

With Ella nosing her arm, Sera inspected the medicine cupboard. Uncapped bottles sat alongside open boxes of tongue depressors, cotton wadding and gauze. "Why hasn't someone run him out of town?"

"He's all we've got, Doc."

"That's not an answer."

"You're desperate, you either drive to Casper or you take your chances with Prichard."

She thought of the pregnant woman she'd spoken to and leaned against the cupboard to close it. "What about midwives?"

"She knows what she's doing."

"Caregivers?"

Crouching, Logan searched out a dusty coffee pot. "You do know where you are, right? You need care, you call a relative, a friend or a neighbor."

She grinned. "Everyone knows everyone, is that it?"

"Pretty much."

"So the Blindfold Killer probably won't risk staying in town."

"Probably not."

"Which leaves campsites, roadside motels… and you've already got that covered, haven't you?"

Logan regarded her from his crouch. "Come here, Sera."

It was his tone more than his expression that had an anticipatory shiver whispering across her skin. No fan stirred the air in the clinic. There was only the heat and her pulse points doing a sudden series of war dances throughout her body.

Stay away, her brain urged. But of course she ignored it and went with the challenge of holding her own against Logan.

"This better turn into a romantic moment because if you show me a dead animal, you'll find you're due for a very nasty vaccination."

"Probably be smarter to take the shot." But his lips curved, and he wrapped his fingers around her neck and held her eyes with his. "This is a really bad idea, Sera."

"I know."

"I can't watch your back if my head's as screwed up as I let it get last night."

"You did? It was?" Delight filtered in. "When? Why? How?"

"Strip poker, strip poker, vivid imagination."

She wanted to laugh, but the urge to kiss him won out, and with a soft "This is so wrong," she took his face in her hands, yanked his mouth onto hers and dived in.

Sensation rocked her from head to toe, wave after stunning wave. A need she hadn't known existed surged and swirled inside her.

It was like plunging head first over a cliff and not knowing if there was water below or a dry roadbed. Not that it mattered. Right then it was all about the fall, about the fiery rush of wind over her limbs and the dark, dangerous taste of him.

Drawing her closer, Logan changed the angle of the kiss, taking it from hot to molten. He used his tongue, his hands and somehow, without moving, his body. There was no gentle exploration this time—there was only greed and hunger and desire, skating on the slippery slope of control.

When his hand slid to her breast, a gasp leaped into her throat. He swallowed it. Sera fisted his hair and nipped his bottom lip. She needed to taste and feel all of him.

She also needed to breathe, and for a heart-thudding moment, she couldn't. Or wasn't. She eased back just far enough to get air and steady her spinning head.

"I feel like I'm on a carousel from hell—only in a good way." Very slowly, the room and her racing heart began to settle. Maybe. Her eyes rose to the ceiling. "Do I hear drums?"

The ghost of a smile crossed Logan's lips. "It's the door, Sera. Someone wants in."

"Ah." Her mouth curved, and she gave his bottom lip a last regretful bite. "For a second I was thinking subarachnoid hemorrhage. Blow to the skull followed by the trauma of a killer kiss." Her smile blossomed when he narrowed his eyes. "One of us should probably answer the door before…"

"Doc Sera, you in there?" A man's voice came from the other side. "It's Travis from last night. Bunch of us out here need looking at."

"Where's a good sub-hem when you need one? Logan, I only wanted to see the clinic. I'm not a family doctor."

"Yes, you are." He gave her a grin and a kiss and brought her back to her feet. "For today anyway." Eyes gleaming, he returned the hat to his head and scratched Ella's ears. "I'll talk to Beth about giving you a hand."

"The Norse nurse?"

"Doc Sera?" the man called again.

"I'll be right there, Travis." She arched meaningful brows. "You realize I need a license to practice medicine in Wyoming."

"I know what you need. I also know you're licensed to practice medicine in seventeen states, one of them being Wyoming. You're running out of arguments, Sera—unless you just don't want to help."

She kept her smile serene as she headed for the door. "It's no wonder you did so well in last night's brawl. Below the belt appears to be your specialty. Talk to Nurse Beth, think of somewhere nice to take me for dinner—your treat as per our poker game bet—and have fun at target practice."

"Sounds like goodbye to me."

"You think?" Then she opened the door to an overflowing waiting room and stopped thinking about anything.

Logan left with a twitch of his lips and, Sera imagined, a satisfied dusting of hands. Trap sprung. His charge was safe, and he was free to pursue other chiefly matters.

Beth arrived within thirty minutes. She wore a beaded headband with a Native American drawing on the front, a feather and leather belt and a ruffled pink blouse.

"I don't like milk," she said and waited as a child might for Sera to respond.

Which she did with a twinkle while inspecting the bullet graze on Toby's right arm. "I don't like green vegetables. Way more problematic."

The young deputy drooped. "I don't like red meat. Try living here and saying that. You think I could go on patrol today, Doc? I mean, moving around's better than sitting behind a desk, right?"

"Depends. How many of your Bulley cousins are in jail now? Four?"

"Five. Logan caught Jake trying to sneak in the back door and jimmy the cell doors."

"People who have turnips for brains do that sort of thing," Beth remarked. "I'll dress that arm if you want to move on, Doctor. Toby's sweet on my granddaughter. He knows I'll only hurt him if he gets her pregnant."

What could she say to that? Sera wondered. With a final inspection, she stepped back. "All yours. I have a possible fractured femur in the next room."

"Any of the local boys get fresh, you tell them I'm here and I brought my enema bag with me."

Sera started out but paused on the threshold. "Toby, do you know if Logan talked to Dr. Prichard about any of this?"

"Prichard's gone fishing, but Logan'll handle him when he gets—ouch—back."

"Sorry." But the sweet-faced Beth didn't look it as she picked up a roll of gauze. "I'm sure that rumor I heard about you and Lily in the movie theater wasn't entirely true."

Grinning, Sera moved on.

One hour flowed into the next. Jenny-Lynn brought her a sandwich and coffee and Ella a bowl of kibble at lunchtime. Then Babe, fresh off the round of flexibility exercises Sera had prescribed, hobbled in wearing a new pair of orthopedic shoes for which she wanted official approval. Ten minutes later, the mayor came by to tell her the gel she'd recommended worked just fine on insect bites.

It was after six o'clock when the last patient appeared. He had his left wrist cradled in his right, and he was pushing his tongue carefully against an incisor.

He watched her in uncertain silence until she walked past him. Then his face cleared. "I know you," he exclaimed. He gave her a sheepish grin. "Recognize your perfume anyway. But I guess it couldn't have been you I saw leaving the bar last night."

Beth poked her head inside. "I'm back with the supplies, Doc. I know we're closing, but I'll just see to the man who's been shuffling his feet on the sidewalk since I left. He's got a lump the size of a duck egg on his skull." She regarded

Sera's patient. "Are you Babe's late husband's cousin Doug?"

The man looked baffled. "Uh, no, ma'am. I'm Roy—Parsons," he added, but he was talking to air as Beth disappeared into the waiting room.

"You get used to it." Sera examined his injured hand. "Is this from a fall or a punch?"

The man's neck went red. "Big guy took a swing at me. I took one back. Felt like I hit a stone wall."

"Sounds like you hit a Bulley." She regarded his swollen knuckles. "Can you move your fingers?"

"Hurts some, but yeah."

With her head bent, she glanced at his face. "You said you saw me leaving the bar last night. Did you see the person with me?"

The red deepened. "Man's about all I can say."

"Can you describe him?"

He shrugged. "Taller than me, maybe six two or so. Thin. Might've had some hair on his face. Mostly I noticed you."

She smiled. "Pretty sure I wasn't walking."

"He had you slung over his shoulder, you know, like firemen do."

"You saw that in the dark?"

He shrugged. "I do a lot of night work up at the construction site, so I'm used to dark. Soon as the lights went out, I closed my eyes and got them adjusted. Opened them and saw you."

"Did you notice anything about the man other than his height?"

Roy Parsons started to shake his head but frowned and wrinkled his nose. "Might've been him who smelled funny. I got a nose for smells. Now, your perfume, that's pretty, but I'm not so fond of mothballs. My old dad, he used to pack everything short of food in them." He wiggled his fingers for her. "I hope you weren't hurt bad, Doc. Some in there were getting mighty loose with their fists."

Beth's head reappeared around the door. "Sorry to interrupt, Dr. Sera, but Fred's here. He's got some kind of musical gizmo for you."

"Five minutes, Beth." Crossing to the medicine cupboard, Sera located a fresh tube of ointment.

She stopped the cap mid-twist as a sudden memory spiked. "Mildew," she murmured.

Her mind flew back. She'd been on the phone. He'd burst in and snatched it away. He'd pushed her. Maybe he'd struck her. She'd gone down. But before things went dark, she'd caught the combined smell of mothballs and mildew. On his coat, she thought now, possibly on that lightweight khaki sleeve as his arm had snaked around her.

The watch was clear enough, worn high on his tanned right wrist. And, yes, it was his sleeve that had smelled of mildew. Like damp, dirty laundry, she reflected now.

"Excuse me, Doc, are you all right?"

Sera blinked and the memory shattered. "Yes—thank you." But her eyes strayed to the door. Logan had said the biker's saddlebags were filled with dirty laundry. He was tall, wiry, probably stronger than he looked. And he'd been at Tommy's bar last night.

The man called Roy slid from the table. "I can come back tomorrow if you're tired."

"What? No, I'm fine." She motioned him back up. "I just got sidetracked for a moment. Can you do me a favor when we're finished here?"

"Don't have to be on site till eight. You got something needs fixing, I'm pretty good with my hands—well, hand."

Behind her, the door leading to the alley slammed open, and a tall man with murderous brown eyes strode in.

His lips peeled away from his teeth when he spied her. Reaching into the back of his pants, he produced a knife, flipped the blade up and whipped it to the underside of her chin.

"Thought you'd be alone by now, Doc, but I'm not figuring on this taking long." He shoved the tip in just deep enough to prick her skin. "No sirree," he snarled. "Not long at all."

Chapter Ten

Sera's heart skipped several beats. She heard Ella bark sharply in the waiting room. The man's small eyes bored into hers. The point of his knife scraped forward under her skin. She spied a movement in her peripheral vision but didn't shift her gaze.

"You're trouble, lady, in big, red letters. All my brothers are behind bars because of you."

"Which would make you the last free Bulley," she replied calmly. "If you want to keep it that way, I'd lose the knife fast."

"Why?" He sneered. "You gonna stick me

with one of your needles, send me to my grave like Doc Prichard did to old Billy's dad?"

Then suspicion crept in. His eyes turned to slits and his mouth snapped shut. Swearing, he started to spin.

Logan blindsided him, catching him by the neck and arm. He might have been the biggest Bulley yet, but he yelped like a girl when his face plowed into the examining table.

"You know I busted a bone in that shoulder last spring, Logan."

"Best cure for a broken bone is a good long rest." With his forearm pressed to the Bulley's neck, Logan regarded Sera. "Did he hurt you?"

Before she could shake her head, Fred and Ella charged through the main door. "You put that knife away, Lester Bulley, or I'll—ah…" Fred spied Logan, and his doubled-up fists relaxed. "Well, that's better."

With the danger passed and Ella growling softly beside her, Sera raised amused brows. "Is this the last of the Bulleys then?"

Logan hauled his captive upright. "There's a couple dozen cousins, aunts and uncles around, but no one who'll want to avenge their so-called honor."

She looked past Fred into the waiting area. Beth was ushering a bandy-legged worker out the door, but otherwise the room was empty.

"I hope he remembers to change the bandage," she remarked.

"If you mean the guy who hightailed it out of here when this one," Fred gave Lester Bulley's ankle a none-too-gentle kick, "broke in, he looked to be wrapped up just fine. Told me there was an apeish Paul Bunyan holding the pretty doc at knifepoint, and if I didn't want her carried off like last night, I should get inside quick."

"Last night." Logan cuffed the seething Bulley and motioned to Fred. "Are we talking potential witness here, Doc?"

"Maybe. The patient's name is Roy Parsons. He saw a tall, thin man carry me out of the bar."

"I'll have Annabelle bring him in. Maybe we can come up with a composite for your assailant's current persona."

"Or maybe, like Clark Kent, he'll duck into a phone booth, whip off his glasses and woo-hoo, unrecognizable."

Logan grinned. "I think our guy probably has a better disguise going than Superman, but any description'll help."

Fred strong-armed the uncooperative prisoner toward the waiting room. "I know you're talking about whoever's after Doc Sera, Logan, but just so you know, I heard some rumbles this afternoon about that biker you ticketed. Don't know where he got it or how, but word is he was out near the Bulley farm today, shooting beer cans off fence posts with a big old semi-automatic gun."

THE RUMOR COULD BE checked. Right then, Logan wanted to talk to Sera's patient. He locked Lester Bulley in with his grumbling brothers, sent Sera and Ella home with Fred and Annabelle out to search for the witness. He recalled her five minutes later when Roy Parsons presented himself at the desk.

"Figured you'd want to see me," he explained, flushing. "Not sure I can help, but I'd be happy to try."

Logan poured him a mug of coffee and phoned Jenny-Lynn at the bar.

"Jen does our composites." He set a hip on one of the desks. "Describe the man you saw, and she'll do a sketch."

It took more than ninety minutes, but when Jenny turned the sketchpad around for the last time, Parson's eyes lit up. "That's him. That's the guy, or mighty close."

Logan thanked him and nodded at Jenny, who gave Roy a tap on the thigh. "Come with me, hon. I'll get you fixed up with dinner and a couple free drinks."

"Dinner anyway. I'm working tonight." The man nodded as he stood. "I hope you find the fellow who hurt the doc. Not right he should go around hitting women."

"Hitting on, yes, hitting, no." Jenny-Lynn left with a wink for Logan and a follow-me swish of her hips for Parsons.

Logan glanced at the clock, made two quick phone calls and turned the station over to his night deputies.

He wanted to head home. Wanted it far more than he should. Dinner out sounded damn good, and he owed Sera a nice one. But he'd been doing battle with his hormones all day, and he suspected it wouldn't take more than a crook of her finger to send his tightly leashed control into a horny tailspin. Better to bolster himself with an extra hour of separation by keeping his mind tuned in to cold, hard fact.

One of those facts involved a phrase no law enforcement officer wanted to hear—copycat killer…

Parsons's description of the current suspect worked in terms of Hugh Paxton's physique, but something about the murderer's MO felt off to him. On the other hand, this was someone chasing down a witness, not looking to fulfill a sick wish.

As he braked at the construction site, Logan spied a scruffy-looking worker on the edge of the gravel lot. The guy was tall, rangy and wearing a three-day growth of beard. Not a ringer for the man in the sketch, but given Paxton's chameleon-like qualities and allowing for witness error, worth a chat.

"You new here?" he asked as the man approached.

Pale eyes flicked to the badge on Logan's waistband. "Thinking 'bout hiring on," he drawled. "Got tools, got a strong back. Figured I'd have a look-see before I talked to the man."

"Where're you from?"

"Speck of a town near Louisville. Don't have a record if that's your real question."

Logan glanced away and kept his tone pleasant. "Record's for Abe to determine. I'm just welcoming a stranger to town."

The man snorted. "Right. You got a smoke?"

"Nope. You got a name?"

"Cody." When Logan merely stared, the man hitched a shoulder. "Jenkins. Hitchhiked here. Got a ride a couple days ago with a guy who was looking to sign on for a few months. Said he was looking to steer clear of his old lady awhile longer."

"So did he sign on?"

"Now how the hell would I know that? Told me his name was Truman if that matters."

"What did he look like?"

"Well, gee, officer, I didn't take notice of his pretty face—seeing as he didn't have tits and his truck smelled like chicken manure. Look, can I go? No law in this state about checking out a prospective employer, is there?"

Logan's lips twitched. "Abe's a good guy. As employers go, a person could do worse."

The man continued walking but with several mistrustful backward glances.

Tucking away what he'd learned, Logan climbed the metal steps to the trailer that served as Abe's project office.

Although it was after 8:00 p.m., the big man was still at his desk. The air smelled of stale cigarettes, coffee and sweat. A slab of raw meat covered his left eye, his shirt was open to the waist and papers were strewn from desk to doorway.

Logan chuckled at his dramatic sprawl. "Bad day?"

"Lost my best welder to a busted finger. Lost my stupid-ass bricklayer to a falling beam. First thing's your fault, second's my assistant's. Got myself a shiner and a gouged shin—also your fault. What is it you want, and do you know anyone who can handle a torch welder?"

"I'll ask around."

Abe squinted at the file Logan held as he spun a chair back to front and straddled it. "If that's paper, don't even think about putting it on my desk." He shifted the meat, cleared his throat. "Is it something I should see?"

Logan tossed a photo onto the pile. "This is from the station's surveillance camera. Have you got a worker named Roy Parsons on your payroll, and is that him?"

Abe blew out a disgruntled breath and worked his way to a semi-upright position. "Yes, I've got a Roy Parsons and yes, that's him. As electricians go, he's decent. Been with me for more'n two months," he added, anticipating Logan's question. "What's that other thing you're holding?"

"Possible serial killer."

Abe's thick fingers recoiled. "Well, hell, I haven't got any of those on my payroll. Pretty sure not, anyway."

"This one might smell like mothballs."

"Unpleasant."

"And mildew."

"Well, now you're talking gross—though I

wouldn't turn down a good welder for a little stink." Turning the meat over, he blew out a breath. "You want me to keep my eyes and nose open and my mouth shut, am I right?"

"Thought crossed my mind."

"I'm surprised there'd be room for thought with the pin-up you got sleeping under your roof." His expression grew sly. "Though maybe not so much sleeping as cold showering, huh?"

"That's real helpful, Abe. Thanks."

"You're a man, aren't you, still breathing?" He drummed the desktop. "What kind of serial killer we talking about here?"

"There's a kind?"

"There's killing, clean and fast, there's raping, mean and nasty and there's butchering, sick and vicious. What does this one do?"

"Clean and fast so far, but MO's change and the victim count's into double digits. You see him, you hear anything, you call me and only me."

Abe pointed to an ancient machine. "Run

me off a copy. I'll keep it in my safe. Dammit, though, Logan, a serial killer, here in Blue Ridge?"

"I'm going to nail this guy, Abe."

"Yeah, but to do that won't he have to try and kill again? And if you don't catch him in the act..." His splayed fingers finished the grisly sentence.

In the corner, the copier made a grinding noise, but it did the job and spit out a replica of Jenny-Lynn's drawing. "The guy's here." Logan handed him the sketch. "And he's out for blood. It's my job to make sure he doesn't get it."

Abe squinted at the composite, then gave his head a dubious shake. "Makes me glad I'm only looking for a welder."

"Now, I NEED to head straight back out." Fred braked his truck at the back of the house. "Flo'll do dinner when you're ready, and I told you what Logan said."

"Yes, he wants a rain check for the poker

game wager his sleight of hand dealing allowed me to win."

"Wouldn't be a gentleman if he'd let you lose even one piece of clothing in a game of strip poker."

Sera smiled and hopped out. "Good night, Fred. Thanks for the iPod. And tell your boss I'm tired, so he can come home any time."

"He's not avoiding you, Doc."

"No, he's just keeping his distance very, very well."

Which was as good for her as it was for him, Sera reminded herself. From the porch, she watched Fred drive into the gathering dusk, then, stretching her cramped shoulder muscles, turned and went inside.

Flo was nowhere to be seen, but raised voices drifting down the third floor stairwell told Sera she was arguing with her daughter.

A warm bath scented with jasmine bubbles soaked away the day's tension. It didn't banish

Logan from her mind, but she doubted anything short of a knockout punch would do that.

Relaxed in the claw-foot tub, she wished for a glass of wine and, if not Logan, then at least an inspired vision. Sleeves and watches were breakthroughs, but until they came with a face, Andi's and Sig's murderer was going to remain free.

Unless he killed again. But even given her limited knowledge of the case, Sera didn't see that happening. He wanted her, and everything she'd seen and heard so far indicated a single-minded man with a very specific purpose.

Resting her head on the curved edge, she let her mind float. Not surprisingly, it went straight to Logan. Strong, silent type, small-town born, drawn to the city and now returned to his rural roots. What had brought him back? Major injury? Doubtful. Sick of the system? Maybe. Lost a partner? Possibly.

He'd lost his uncle in any case. His uncle and

his friend. What else might he lose before this was over?

"Okay, not going there," she told herself and, shaking off the haze, plugged into the iPod Fred had loaned her. Bob Marley's "One Love" was on the playlist, but her only memory now had to do with Logan and how hot he'd looked in his cop clothes.

She listened on as she traded water and bubbles for a pair of faded jeans and a black tank.

Ella was snoring on the bedroom floor. When Sera clapped her hands, the dog's head sprang up, and she gave two excited barks.

"Wanna run?" She grinned when Ella's tail began to wag. "Thought so. Come on, then. You deserve some freedom after being cooped up in a waiting room all day."

The retriever raced into the darkness the moment Sera opened the screen door downstairs.

She smelled spaghetti sauce and wondered if she was supposed to eat or wait for Flo. She was dipping a spoon in the spicy sauce when the housekeeper marched into the kitchen, thin-lipped and obviously displeased.

Because there was no point pretending, Sera asked, "How's Autumn?"

Flo set a large pot of water on the stove. "She left thirty minutes ago—took off in my old clunker while my back was turned. Must've hot-wired it. I hate to think where she picked that up. Girl needs an intervention, you ask me."

"Would she be receptive to it?"

"Does she need to be?"

"Makes it easier but, no, she doesn't. I've only been involved in a few. One went well then fell apart, second was a disaster from the start, and the third started badly but turned."

Flo dropped a double handful of noodles into the pot. "Define the word 'disaster.'"

"The man died two months after he was removed from his residence."

"Drugs or alcohol?"

"Old age mostly. Dementia, coupled with a troubled life. Was Autumn a troubled child?"

"She was thirteen when she slept with her first Bulley. Fourteen when she used her first needle." There was a long pause while Flo tracked and swatted a fly. "Speaking of intervention and dementia, Edgar Bulley's sister hasn't been right for some time. Sits in her attic room at the farmhouse, rocks and knits and sings old Patsy Cline songs. Once when I went up to visit her, I started to take her needles away so she could eat, and she stabbed my leg. A few seconds later, she went back to knitting and singing like nothing had happened."

"And Dr. Prichard said…?"

"She needed a vitamin shot."

Sera would have laughed if the woman's condition hadn't sounded so serious. "Edgar Bulley would be the relative to approach. If he agrees, the process could be initiated."

"A complicated process?"

"Can be. It depends on the individual involved and how dangerous the afflicted person is. Resistance and borderline competency can make things—well, sticky."

A deep rumble sounded in the distance.

"Storm coming," Flo predicted. Her mouth compressed to a line. "My clunker doesn't run in the rain. Do the girl good to spend a night stranded on the side of the road. She knows not to bring her drugs here, but she does it anyway. How many times can we expect Logan to look the other way?" She plated the noodles with a vengeance and ladled chunky marinara sauce on top. "Eat," she ordered in a no-nonsense tone. "You've had a long day, and you're too thin. Your mother should've pushed you harder."

"Oh, she pushed plenty hard, Flo."

"You don't like her?"

"Not particularly. By the Freudian yardstick, I love her because she's my mother, but like her? Not by any measure." Sera's eyes rose as the lights flickered. "That's not promising."

"There's a generator."

The housekeeper surprised her by bringing her own full plate to the table. Then she realized why and acceptance came out in a sigh. "Logan told you to watch me, didn't he?"

"Suggested it." Flo passed a plate of warm breadsticks. "I had no argument. He's a fine man, our chief. Got some history of his own."

"Do you know why he left L.A.?"

"Not the specifics, but he had that look cops get when their defenses are running down. Pain starts to sneak in. Sometimes other feelings break loose."

Sera stopped twirling as thunder rattled the walls of the old house. "That's close. Has there been anyone special since he came to Blue Ridge?"

"Nope."

She smiled a little at the housekeeper's tone. "I'm not trying to pry, Flo."

"Yes you are. Wouldn't be a woman if not. Logan came here looking for something. Came looking to put something else behind him. I figure he's about halfway done with both things. Could be the right woman'll speed matters along, but being right means being open. Life's full of peaks and valleys. You've gotta roll to get through them in one piece. Me, I rock better than I roll, but Fred taught me how to combine the two. Seems like now it's your turn to do the same. Your choice anyway."

How had this shifted from Logan to her? Scraping her chair back, Sera went to the stove for more sauce. "I've made a lot of choices already in my life. Being in Blue Ridge wasn't one of them."

"Got a stalker after you, I hear."

"You hear very well."

"Logan'll catch him."

"Promise?"

She was dipping the ladle into the pot when the overhead lights snapped off. No flicker of warning, just off.

Sera tried to ignore the finger of fear that slid

along her spine. "Please tell me the generator's not in the cellar."

"Nope." Flo's voice came from across the room. "In the barn."

"Well, I feel better."

"A little dark won't hurt me."

"Us," Sera corrected.

"If you want. Flashlight's in the mudroom."

"It would be." The blackness was so complete, she had to feel her way along the kitchen wall.

"Emergency gear's on the right, second shelf."

"Like I can see the shelves to count them," Sera muttered. But she located the door and re-membered to step down.

She groped through a variety of jars and bot-tles before she reached the metal-cased light. "Found it," she called in.

"Got another one here," Flo returned. Then she made a sound of disgust. "Oh, now who left the door open? Fred are you home? I swear, if your shoes are muddy…"

Sera was testing her beam when the house-keeper broke off. Fear tickled her throat. "Flo?"

There was no answer.

She tried again, louder and with tension beginning to thrum. "Flo, are you all right?"

A bolt of lightning shot through the sky beyond the barn. On its heels, thunder rocked the foundation of the farmhouse.

Unless it had been Fred at the door and he'd swept his wife into a passionate embrace—unlikely from what Sera had seen—something was wrong.

Acting quickly, she scanned the shelves. On the highest one she found a box of bullets and an old .32 caliber gun.

There was a phone on a stand behind the door. Controlling her fear, she punched Logan's cell number. Then she wedged the handset between her shoulder and ear and shoved bullets into the empty chamber.

"Yeah, this is Logan."

"Where are you?" she demanded without preface.

"A mile south of the Bulley farm. What's wrong?"

"I'm not sure. The power went out. Flo and I split up to look for flashlights. She said something about someone coming in—through the side door, I think—then suddenly, she stopped talking."

"Is Ella there?"

Braced for his reaction, Sera shoved the last bullet in place. "I let her out for a run. I don't know where she is." She heard Logan's low curse and almost smiled.

"Where are you now?"

"Mudroom. I've got a gun. I'm going to look for Flo."

"Sera, don't…"

"There's no don't, Logan. For all I know, she fell and hit her head."

"You've met her, right? Stay where you are. Don't go looking for Flo or the generator."

More lightning forked through the sky. Sera glanced up. Then slowly down as something caught her eye.

Her heart, already hammering, sank into her stomach. "Oh, hell," she breathed.

"What?"

"I'm looking at the barn, Logan, in the alcove above the door. There's a light on."

Chapter Eleven

The power hadn't failed. Someone had cut the line to the house. Or worse, switched off the breakers from the inside.

Panic would have blocked all thought if Sera hadn't mastered the art of breathing through it as a child. Block nerves and focus on what was good.

Her eyes were adjusting. And she knew how to shoot. All she had to do was keep her back to a wall so whoever had cut the power couldn't ambush her.

Fear slowly gave way to determination. This madman would not take another innocent life.

If Flo was alive, she was going to stay that way. They'd get out of here together or not at all.

With her gun pointed at the floor, Sera stepped up into the house. The thunder outside sounded like cannonfire. The darkness in the kitchen was thick and menacing, the air still and eerily silent.

She worked her way across the large room toward the pantry. "Flo?" she whispered.

Nothing stirred. Flo didn't answer.

Hugging the wall, Sera shone her light into the pantry. No Flo. But she spied clumps of dirt, the kind that came in on the soles of shoes, so someone had been here. Undoubtedly still was.

She breathed in and turned the beam back to the kitchen.

The swinging door presented a huge mental barrier. Releasing her breath, she gripped the gun and pushed through to the hallway. "Flo?"

A barely audible scrape halted her. On its heels, she caught a low creak, not directly ahead but somewhere on the ground floor.

Angry drops of rain spit fretfully against the windows. The thunder and lightning were almost simultaneous now. In the flashes, she saw Andi's lifeless face, then Sig's and finally, the hazy outline of a man. Real or imagined? In her mind, she saw his gloved hands reaching for her...

"Doc Sera?"

The image dissolved as a smaller pair of hands clutched her arm. A head toppled against her shoulder, and the body beneath it sagged.

"Flo!" Sera caught the woman before her knees buckled. "What happened? Did someone hit you?"

"From behind." The housekeeper's fingers dug in deep. "Room went black. When I came to, I was alone, but I don't think he's gone."

"So we'll go instead. Where's the closest door?"

"Front, but I heard a creak that way."

Sera kept her on her feet. "Second closest?"

"Back through the kitchen—unless we go

into the cellar. Not sure I can make it down the stairs."

Making it down was a moot point as far as Sera was concerned. No way was she trapping herself in a dark, dank basement with a serial killer behind her.

"Let's go with the kitchen." Wrapping an arm around Flo's waist, she hoisted and gently pushed. "Logan's on his..." This time it wasn't a creak so much as a footstep that reached them. "...way. Did that come from the living room?"

"Might have. My ears are ringing."

Sera bumped against the banister. Up wasn't smart, but what choice did they have?

"Dr. Hudson?" A man's voice whispered her name. "Are you hiding in the dark, hoping I'll go away? Do you know me? Remember me? Remember any of it?"

Sera could barely hear him above the rain and thunder, but he felt close, as if he was breathing down her neck.

"I don't know where he is," she told Flo. "We have to go up."

The housekeeper nodded.

They went backward a step at a time. In the spread of darkness below, the killer chuckled.

"I have a bandanna ready for you, Dr. Sera. Hospital white. Sterile. Fools rush in, but some fools see nothing. They just close their eyes and jump."

"What's he saying?" Flo grunted.

"Shhh." Sera glanced upward. They'd climbed ten stairs. Four to go. Unless he rushed. Her heart gave a hard slam, but she kept moving. Two stairs left. And there it was, the upper landing.

"I'll find you, Doctor," he warned and chuckled again. "I'll simply turn the lights back on, and there you'll be. Beautiful as life and twice as deadly. The Hippocratic hypocrite."

Sera started along the hall. Where to? Flo was in no condition to shimmy down a trellis. She was trying to decide what to do when watery headlights swept across the wall beside her.

"Thank God." She breathed out. "Logan's here."

The housekeeper's head lolled sideways. "Going under," she mumbled. "Get to Logan's room. Best place. Big window. Should be able to climb down."

Sera didn't argue. Did she hear measured footsteps on the stairs? Maybe the killer hadn't spotted the headlights.

The door opened silently. The window faced the front of the house. If she could get to it, she could call down to Logan.

Depositing Flo in a chair, she ran. She was halfway across the floor when something surged up to her right. She felt a wet draft a split second before a body crashed into her side and sent her flying onto the bed.

Dodging a balled fist, she brought her knee up and used the gun she still carried to slam his ear. When he yelped, she kneed him again and rolled off the bed.

She landed on all fours on the plank floor. Righting herself quickly, she planted her forearms on the mattress and aimed at the doubled over silhouette darting for the door.

She went for his leg, heard the bullet embed itself in wood and fired again. A sharp zing told her the shot had ricocheted.

The door opened. Feet pounded. Then they stopped and thudded back again. The silhouette darted past the bed and vanished through the open window.

Sera let her head fall onto her outstretched arms. "Flo?"

"Still here." She sounded weak but aware. "Logan must be downstairs. Guess you showed that scumbag a thing or two."

Sera forced her head partway up. "Scared him anyway." While her heart searched for a semi-steady beat, she rested her chin on her arm and let the obvious question creep in.

The killer had been on the first floor when she and Flo had started up the stairs. So how, she wondered, had he gotten into Logan's bedroom ahead of them?

"FLO'S FINE. SHE'S asleep," Logan said to Fred in the kitchen.

The lights were back on and Sera and Flo were safe. No thanks to him, Logan reflected with a thrust of self-directed anger. The Blindfold Killer had escaped again. Barely, but he'd done it, roared off in a cloud of rain and dust and sporting, he hoped, a crippled groin.

"How'd he do it?" Fred wanted to know. "Sera said he was threatening them down here, then suddenly, he was up in your room."

Logan braced his hands on the counter. "I checked the trellis. There's a lot of damage, and the window was only open a crack when I left this morning. Sera swears it was wide open when the guy jumped through it."

"So he used the trellis to get upstairs ahead of them?"

"It's one possibility."

Fred rubbed a guilty palm over his head and paced circles around the table. "I should've gotten Annabelle to look into that break and enter down the road. Only take a minute, I thought. But then my engine overheated, and Ginny Bulley doesn't answer her phone after hours. What if they'd been killed, Logan? Whose fault would that have been?"

"Not yours." Pushing off, Logan went to the fridge, pulled out a beer and tossed it to his distraught deputy. "Sera fired, the guy took off and I'm the one who should be kicking himself because this is the second time I've missed him."

"You weren't supposed to be here. I was. Fault's mine."

Logan debated, then thought to hell with it and pulled another beer. "We could do this dance all night, Fred, but the fact is, I'm the chief of police in Blue Ridge. Sera's safety is my responsibility. End of story."

"End of fairy tale, more like." Arms folded, Sera leaned against the frame. She held the swinging door open with her shoulder and regarded them through mildly exasperated green eyes. "My life and safety are my own responsibility, gentlemen—and especially Logan. While I appreciate the effort everyone's making—again, especially Logan—I'm not a five-year-old child who requires constant supervision. People with goals, good and or evil, generally find a way to fulfill them. If one of you had been here tonight, he might not have done what he did, but you know he'd have done something at some point and maybe then, instead of failing, he'd have succeeded, and this conversation would look good by comparison."

Logan let a faint smile escape as he handed her his beer. "Sounds like the twisted logic of a tired shrink to me."

"Tired's better than dead." Fred glanced upward. "Can I see Flo?"

"She's sleeping, but yes, you can. There's no sign of concussion. I'll check her through the night and tomorrow. It wasn't your fault, Fred," she added as he squeezed past her.

A gusty expulsion of breath was his only response before he clomped up the stairs.

"And then there were two." She said it with a twinkle that amazed Logan almost as much as it confounded him. Was there anything a shrink couldn't or wouldn't rationalize?

Taking the beer back, he walked away, tipped the bottle for a long swallow. "Any point in me repeating that you could have been killed tonight?"

"What, because I'm not under the bed quaking with fear, you think I don't know that?"

"I have no idea what you do or don't know, Sera. I know I was thirty-five when I left here this morning, and I'm at least ten years older now. Beyond that—" He drank again. "—not a clue."

"Then let me clue you in. Being scared pisses me off. Being pissed off makes me cranky. It's a chain reaction that winds itself around to simply getting through or past whatever's necessary in order to come out whole at the other end."

Giving the door a shove, she came toward him. Her footsteps might be measured, but her expression verged on dangerous.

Now why the hell, he wondered in mild annoyance, should that excite him?

The storm outside had circled. The atmosphere in the kitchen felt electric. He hadn't turned on many lights, mostly because he preferred a stark atmosphere. The resulting shadows heightened the tension in the room and made his already heated blood pump with more force than was probably healthy.

Facing her across the table, he gave his beer a slow swirl. "Do you know who you're dealing with, Sera?"

Her brows went up. "Are we talking about you or the Blindfold Killer?"

"I want this guy, and I'm going to get him. He wants you, and that's not going to happen. You'd think somewhere in that tangle, we'd find some common ground."

A glimmer he didn't need to see swam up into her green eyes. "Are you trying to defuse my really workable irritation-born-of-fear mood by suggesting that we might be able to work together?"

He half smiled. "Believe me, Doc, it goes against the grain, but not knowing every last detail of the current case puts me at a disadvantage. I've got what Sig had in his files, but I don't have what was in his head. And I sure as hell don't have a window into the Blindfold Killer's mind."

"So enter Mata Hari?" She started around the table, with a seductive walk that was sixty percent female and forty percent nitro.

He didn't reach out and haul her in as she approached, but it was a close thing. Setting the bottle aside, he let her stroke a finger over his cheek to the corner of his mouth.

"And still he resists. You're a man of spectacular control, Logan."

He held her eyes even as his own began to glitter. "You think?" And giving in, let the last threads of his restraint snap.

He crushed his mouth to hers in a kiss that wanted to punish as much as pleasure. Not her but him. Sensation swept in on a swell of emotions so strong he wondered how he'd ever managed to bury them.

He used his tongue to explore, his lips to taste, his hands to discover. When she pressed herself into him, he was already rock hard.

Her hands fisted in the ends of his hair and tugged. She nipped at his mouth, tempting him to take her right there, in the middle of the kitchen, in the middle of the night.

He ran his lips over her cheek to her ear and along the side of her neck. Somewhere in the jumble of need and greed and hunger, he expected to feel the raw edge of pain. Or guilt. Something that would sweep in and blacken the moment or at least sucker punch the hell out of it.

He felt her smile against his mouth and heard the sound she made in her throat. She hooked her arms around his neck. "Just a little rough there, Logan." But when he drew back, she gave his lip a quick bite. "I like it," she said. And dived back in.

Without the threads, Logan knew he was alone on the slippery edge. It started or ended here. He could ease away or take the plunge. His edge. His choice.

Smiling, she drew back far enough to tease, then with a velvet purr, jumped up to wrap her legs around his hips.

Every scrap of sanity flew out the window.

The crash he heard on the edge of his mind might have been thunder or something shattering inside. He'd have put it down to the last thing if the swinging door hadn't suddenly banged off the kitchen wall and jolted them apart.

Fred barreled in, shirtless and gesturing wildly. "I think a tree just fell on the barn."

Shoving his brain back in gear, Logan joined his deputy at the window. And swore. "That wasn't a tree."

Fred squinted. "Roof looks to be intact all right."

"It wasn't a tree," Logan repeated and handed Sera his cell. "Find Zack Walter's number. He's the volunteer fire chief. Then get your medical bag."

Already scrolling, she attempted to peer past him. "What is it? What happened?"

"Lightning hit the side," Fred declared. "I see flames."

"It wasn't lightning. It was a car." Logan headed for the door. "Bag, Sera."

Fred blinked. "Someone's car hit the barn?"

"Not someone's car." Logan grabbed the fire extinguisher from the mudroom shelf. "Flo's."

Chapter Twelve

Amazingly, Autumn wasn't injured, not in the crash or in the fire that broke out when sparks ignited the fuel leaking from Flo's rusty tank. But her breath smelled of whiskey, her pupils were dilated and she muttered "Dumb hick" the whole time Sera was examining her.

It took an hour to extinguish the flames, but less than half that to assess the damage. Fred moaned, Logan talked to the fire chief and Flo slept on unaware.

Sera took Autumn upstairs, undressed and covered her, then checked her vitals again.

Being drunk and high, she figured the woman would sleep like the dead until she surfaced.

To punish himself for his daughter's misdeeds, Fred stationed himself at Sera's bedroom door for the remainder of the night. He refused to let her out of his sight the next day, even when cars and trucks began pulling up at the front gate. Apparently no clinic in town meant the patients she hadn't seen yesterday would come to her.

She palpated ribs, examined arthritic joints and treated a variety of peculiar rashes. Beth drove out mid-morning to help. She wore a bright smile and cowboy boots and toted two large platters of brownies.

The thunderstorm moved on and the sun returned. The temperature soared to ninety-four degrees. By six o'clock, Sera was ready to follow Autumn's lead, steal Fred's truck and head for Alaska.

Her fingers sticky with frosting, Beth finally closed and locked the door.

"Clinic's done," she declared. "You tell Logan

I'll send my son out here tomorrow to see about repairing his barn."

Fred shook the offer away. "I'll do it. Logan's being too nice not charging Autumn with anything."

Beth poked a chocolate-tipped finger into his chest. "And just what do you know about carpentry, Deputy Fife?"

"Enough to patch a barn." Fred snatched up his fifth brownie. "Back me up here, Doc."

"Taking the Fifth." She released her hair from its ponytail and headed for the swinging door. "I'm going to find a rock and watch the sun set. I'll take Ella," she added, grinning. "And I'll stay where you can see me."

"Do that," Fred warned. "Because I know for a fact that two of the Bulley boys were cut loose last night, and time's up on a third one tonight."

She patted his arm before she left. "Stop beating yourself up, Deputy. Moon Flower will be her usual sanguine self tomorrow. Poof." She spread her fingers in a starburst. "Worry bubble popped."

Rolling a cramp from her shoulder, she left Beth to badger him out of his funk. After washing up and snagging a Diet Coke from the fridge, she wandered into the backyard. Ella trotted dutifully behind her. The moment Sera settled on a rock, the dog flopped down to bask in the waning rays of sunlight.

The Big Horns rose clear and craggy in the distance, and for the first time all day, a breeze fluttered across Sera's cheeks.

Normal, she thought and smiled at the concept that somehow always eluded her.

The B movie of her childhood began to play in her head. Sparkles everywhere. Puff up the hair, strut, smile, own the stage, work the room. Don't smudge the makeup, flash the spray tan. Watch out for strap lines.

She paused there, her gaze on a fluffy white cloud. A man's arm appeared, but there was no khaki sleeve and no chrome watch. There was only a mark, a tan line where a watch should have been.

The image came and went in a heartbeat. Was it important, she wondered, or was she grasping at memory straws that meant nothing in the grand scheme?

Reclining on her elbows, she tried to empty her mind. Logan snuck in, but she was used to that and worked around him.

She brought back the smells, mildew and mothballs, and the sound—Bob Marley on Andi's computer—the arm, the sleeve, the watch, the grimace…

With the soda bottle poised at her mouth, she zeroed in on the last thing and saw it again. Gloved hands reaching, teeth clenched and bared.

They weren't particularly white teeth, and the lower front ones were crooked.

"Okay…" She drew the word out. "That's a good sign." A second later, her instincts kicked in, and a smile flitted across her lips. "Oh, yeah, really good."

At her side, Ella rolled over, blissfully unconcerned.

Sera counted down from five. As a shadow fell over her, she gripped the knife she'd taken from the kitchen and brought it around Bulley style so the tip touched the underside of a man's chin.

"Well, hey there, Chief," she greeted. Then using the tip to draw him forward, she set her mouth on his.

SERA KNEW LOGAN was up to something when he suggested they eat at Frank's Diner. He wasn't paying her back for the dinner he owed her, and, although he might be disarming her from across the table, she wasn't foolish enough to read this as a romantic whim on his part. Still, if he wanted to bide his time, she could play along.

While Tim McGraw spun on the jukebox, she

indicated a man at the bar. "I recognize him from the other night."

"That's Travis. He's Abe's foreman."

"The guy he's talking to, the one with the curly brown hair and leathery skin, looks familiar, too. Probably from the clinic. And there's good old Wayne, the biker with the dirty laundry. No chance he's the Blindfold Killer, huh?"

"He's not Hugh Paxton if that's what you mean."

Something in Logan's tone brought her gaze to his shadowed face. "Isn't one the same as the other?"

"Maybe."

"Oh good, now you're going all mysterious on me. Please say you're not thinking that someone's copying the killer's MO."

"If someone is, he's copying details that weren't released to the media."

"For example?"

"The particular way the bandanna's folded. The fact that the Blindfold Killer always makes sure his victim's eyes are open and they're found lying face up."

"Why do I sense puzzlement?"

"Unlike the previous eleven, three of the four recent victims, Sig and his partner not included, had their wrists bound with red tape."

"That's very interesting." She drew a circle inside a square on the table. "I assume the one not bound was Andi. Because I interrupted him?"

"Possibly."

"You're being mysterious again, Chief. Any chance of an explanation?"

"Yeah. When I have one that works." He looked at the door. "Do you recognize those men who just came in?"

She had to squint through a sea of brawny bodies. "No, should I?"

"They're two of the new workers Abe took on right after Sig was killed."

"And?"

"They have alibis. One by his wife, the other

by a maid and a motel clerk in Buffalo. People lie, though. It never hurts to double-check. Third guy on Abe's list ditched the site before I could talk to him."

"Does that say 'bad guy' to a cop?"

"It says question mark. The description I got was of an average-looking, forty-something male, several inches above average height."

Propping her elbows on the table, Sera pressed on her temples. "I think my head hurts." But she slid her eyes to the man standing next to Travis. "Maybe he's the one who's supposed to come back for a tetanus shot."

"Don't count on him keeping the appointment if he is."

Logan's expression made her laugh. "That's so cool. You went green at the thought. Tells me where your Achilles heel is—should I ever need to find it."

"You won't."

As Tim segued to Steve Earle, Sera's amusement faded. "You didn't bring me here so we could guess our way to the Blindfold Killer's identity, Logan. I sense an ulterior motive, and whatever it is, I sense much more strongly that I'm not going to like it."

"You're a perceptive woman." Sitting back, he rested a forearm on the table. "Okay, here's the deal. I know a guy. His name's Hollis. I met him in L.A., somewhere between Vice and Homicide. He was quirky, but he got results, and that's all the department cared about."

"What kind of results and how quirky?"

Trapping her fingers, he rubbed a thumb over her knuckles. "Hollis lives in a trailer near a town called Starlight."

"Sounds pretty."

"Depends on your definition."

"Okay, not so pretty. Why?"

"Am I telling you about him?"

"Oh, no, I'm way past that. You want me to meet him. What I want to know is why, and—going out on a limb here, Chief—how it is you think he can help me smash through the wall in my head. Please say he's not a psychic."

"First six letters are right. He's a psychiatrist."

She stared in genuine surprise. "But you hate them—us."

"Having a problem with something or someone doesn't equal hate. Hollis is a friend first and foremost. I was on my way to see him two years ago when I stopped in Blue Ridge."

An intriguing statement. However… "Logan, if I thought a psychiatrist could help me, I know half a hundred reputable ones in California. What I really need is a mind reader. Or maybe another whack on the head."

He took a drink of the beer a harried Nadine plopped down at his elbow. "Hollis is a shrink, but his strong suit is hypnotism."

"Whoa." In a knee-jerk reaction, Sera jumped back in her chair. "Forget it. I mean, I have nothing against hypnotherapy. It has its place, and I've seen several cases where it's worked."

"But?"

"My mind, my memory, my call." Five tense seconds ticked by before she offered a grudging, "What kind of results does he get, percentage-wise, I mean?"

Grinning slightly, Logan captured her chin. "What you really want to know is why he lives in a trailer in the back of beyond."

"Well, duh, Chief, wouldn't you? I'm picturing Brother Love here."

"You think I'd ask you to turn your mind over to a man who sells potions out of a fifth wheel?"

Although her blood was heating up, she didn't pull free. "We called them POHs in college. Professors of Hypnotology. Shysters who staged sideshow seminars to hoodwink gullible audience members into purchasing their expensive DVD collections. No, I don't think you'd take me to someone like that, but come on, Logan, a trailer in the woods? That's not quirky—that's weird."

"He graduated top of his class from Harvard."

"Even more weird."

"Rumor has it he's worked with politicians and royals."

"So having achieved such lofty goals, it makes perfect sense he'd go all mountain man and withdraw from the world."

"You're scared of being hypnotized, aren't you?"

"No—yes. Maybe." She tried not to hiss. "It's that control thing I told you about. I don't like relinquishing it, even to a Harvard grad." But her resistance wavered as her curiosity deepened. "Is it far to Starlight?"

"Four-hour drive. We can be there by midnight."

She flicked a disbelieving finger. "Midnight—as in you want to do this tonight?"

He drew her closer until all she could see were his unfathomable eyes. "I want this to end, Sera. Now. Before your luck and mine run out. In one form or another, the Blindfold Killer's here in Blue Ridge, and he's losing what little patience he might have had."

Fear rose like bile in Sera's throat, but she held his gaze and refused to let it win. "Something's happened," she said. "Tell me, Logan, before the freak-out I'm having in my head spreads to the rest of my body."

He stared a moment longer, then reached into his shirt pocket and removed a folded paper. "I found this taped to the house after the excitement died down last night."

She didn't want to see it, really didn't want to know. But she made herself take the paper and read the killer's chilling words.

Those who cannot see
never will again.
When fools rush in,
sometimes the angel they meet
is armed.
I am the Angel of Vengeance,
Sera Hudson.
And you are DEAD!!

Chapter Thirteen

Logan didn't speak, just ran a contemplative finger under his lower lip and glanced at her from time to time as they drove north.

He knew when to leave someone alone. Before he'd resigned from the force, his captain and several other well-meaning superiors had pushed, prodded and finally ordered him to talk. Instead, he'd retreated into full stony silence. Two weeks later he'd packed up his truck and started driving.

Although he still wasn't sure how he'd wound up in Blue Ridge, living here for two plus years had worked for him. Then Sig had called, and the fabric of his new life had begun to shred.

He didn't want to care about Sera or any woman. Regardless of where you started, caring invariably led you to despair. But that was only the first stop on the road. Final destination? Hotel California every time.

They'd been off the interstate for thirty minutes before she shot him a vexed look. "You know, Logan, it's possible I didn't have a clear view of the murderer's face. It was dark, it was raining, Andi and I were alone in the office. We had our desk lights and computers on but not much else."

His lips curved. "You remember scratches on a chrome watch, Sera. You could see well enough."

She plucked a pine needle from the leg of her capris. Designer label, he reminded himself. Like the snug white halter top she wore and the green jacket she carried.

"I feel like there's something else, something

connected to that watch." She fanned her fingers across the windshield. "I know it's out there in the vast universe that's my memory. I'm just not sure if this particular thing's blocked or simply eluding me."

"Is this thing more recent than your friend's death?"

"Feels like it."

He sent her a considering look. "It's possible you've seen the Blindfold Killer in Blue Ridge, and what your conscious mind didn't recognize, your subconscious one did."

She grinned for the first time since getting in his truck. "My how you've changed, Dr. Jung. Much hotter this time around. Definitely more persuasive."

"Sera, Hollis isn't going to make you cluck like a chicken every time you hear a bell."

She narrowed her eyes at him.

He knew better than to chuckle. "This is a good idea. Why are you fighting so hard?"

"Well, hmm, let me think. Maybe because it's me?"

His lips quirked. "Yeah, I've heard doctors make crappy patients."

"Given a choice, Logan, which would you prefer, a tetanus shot or turning your mind over to a stranger?"

"Stranger hands down."

"Uh-huh."

"I hate needles."

"Fine, you get hypnotized, I'll take the shot."

He continued to check his amusement. "Are you always so difficult in circumstances like this?"

"I wouldn't know, I've never been in circumstances like this. You could at least let me test out my whack-on-the-head idea first."

"You already have." He turned off the rutted road onto a strip of dirt hardly wider than a cow path. "Barroom brawl, Sera. You wound up in the backseat of a truck stolen from Edgar Bulley's farm. Remember?"

She sighed. "At least *you* let me pack an overnight bag." She drew a vague air sketch. "Tell me, do you know why one of the side windows in Edgar Bulley's truck has Lamont Cranston as The Shadow painted on it?"

Frowning, Logan glanced over. "There's no Lamont Cranston in Edgar's truck, Sera."

"No? Huh. Well, whoever it was it looked like my childhood recollection of Lamont." She let her hand drop. "My uncle Geoffrey has a collection of old Shadow tapes."

"Sera, there's nothing painted anywhere on Edgar's truck. The body itself is more than half rust."

"Look, I know I saw…" She trailed off, reconsidered. "Maybe not a drawing." Her eyes came up. "Maybe a tattoo. On the Blindfold Killer's—" her fingers danced from side to side "—left shoulder. His shirt was torn, or coming apart at the seam."

"Are we talking about the night he murdered

your friend, or the night he carried you out of the bar?"

She ran both scenarios. "I'm going to speculate that the truck memory is transference. When I think Shadow, I see a khaki coat." Clearly frustrated, she huffed out a breath. "Maybe this hypnotism thing's not a bad idea after all. Just please don't let him take me into my childhood."

A dark brow went up. "Afraid of what you might find, Doc?"

"More afraid of what I might say."

"So you'd rather die than risk an unconnected revelation."

Before she could respond, a lopsided trailer came into view. Around them the trees and towering boulders gave way to a tiny mountain clearing. But her gaze wasn't fixed on the trailer. Instead, she watched an enormous bearded man walk slowly toward them. He had an ax in one hand and a burlap bag in the other.

"There's a sight you don't see every day," she managed. "Grizzly Adams on steroids."

"That's not Grizzly Adams." Logan shoved the door of his truck open. "And it's not Hollis either."

"I SWEAR, MICHAEL Logan, you were born suspicious." A man with a long gray beard and features much finer than those of the hulk outside smiled benignly as he handed Sera a cup of tea. "Drink up, Doctor." He winked. "It's my own special blend."

"Black tea and bats' wings?" she countered with a twinkle.

He chuckled. "Chamomile and rose hips actually. For tranquility and trust. Although," he glanced at Logan, "I think you brought your own trust with you. If it sets your mind at ease, I'll tell you that man outside was gathering mushrooms for soup. He insists they taste best if they're collected at night. Never mind about the ax. Moving on, Logan informs me you're having a problem accessing a certain pivotal memory. I hope it won't shake your confidence if I tell you I've had that same problem on a near-daily basis since becoming an octogenarian."

Sera regarded him in amazement. "You're eighty years old? I would never have guessed that."

"Which could be a compliment or not, as I recently celebrated my eighty-seventh birthday. Thank you again for the satellite phone, Logan." His blue eyes sparkled. "The boy worries."

"I've noticed."

"To business, then." He removed a watch from his shirt pocket, noted Sera's reaction and chuckled again. "Simply checking the time, Doctor. I'm something of a night owl. I do my best work in the wee hours. Used to drive the police and my colleagues crazy."

He had a very soothing voice. Coupled with the serenity of his manner and the comforting sight of the half million books he had crammed in his trailer, Sera imagined he would have little trouble taking a person under.

Pushing aside a strand of gray hair, he tapped the multifaceted crystal earring that dangled from his left lobe.

"Focus on the center, Sera. A crystal is a maze of planes and angles, but the mind is far more complex. What can't be accessed from one direction must be approached from another."

Sera knew she could resist, and for a moment she almost did. But if she never remembered that horrible night, Andi and Sig's killer would remain at large, free to murder again.

Taking a deep breath, she focused on the crystal.

As if drawn by a magnet, her mind moved toward the glittering center. She saw faces reflected in the facets—Logan's, Fred's, Jenny-Lynn's, a cluster of Bulleys'.

She heard the roar of a motorcycle, the same sound as last night. Dirty Laundry Wayne rode an old Kawasaki. He had an attitude and the word "nasty" stamped on every feature. But Logan said he wasn't Hugh Paxton, and she believed him. She might even…

No, stop. Not going there.

Switching directions, she let her mind tiptoe through a welter of memories, some nice, some not. When the mist surrounding them cleared, she was in her office.

It was dark, after hours. She'd had a difficult day. The police wanted an evaluation done on one of their own. She'd have to squeeze that in. And an Oakland social worker named Jody Frost wanted to talk to her.

She had called thirty minutes after the office closed. She'd just returned from a funeral. She said it was urgent. Sera mentally penciled her in for late the following day.

"I'm going down to the deli," Andi called from reception. "I've been sorting through our inactive files. That old guy of yours with the freako son died last Christmas, right? His name was Gould, Harvey or Henry."

Sera scrolled through a current patient file. "It was Harvey," she called back. "He died two days after Thanksgiving."

"What about Ballard? And Tristan Teas?"

"Those were your patients, Andi."

"Yes, but your memory's better than mine. Really, you should be going through this stuff. Come on, Ballard and Teas, dead or alive?"

"Both gone. Ballard died nine months ago in state prison. Teas committed suicide in February."

"We're not having much patient luck, are we?" Andi's voice began to fade. "Sometimes our job sucks."

A door closed. Rain streamed down the office window. In the distance, the Golden Gate Bridge was slowly being consumed by fog. Meant the rain was moving on. Beneath her fingers, the computer keyboard went dark.

Suddenly, she had a patient chart in her hand.

The outer door closed again. "I'm back," Andi called. "Now before you tell me off, I'm sorry about the wet, but I didn't come prepared today."

Already immersed in the chart, Sera only half heard her. She started for the door, still scanning. "Andi, this patient's…"

A desk lamp burned in front of her. Did she look straight at it? Is that why she couldn't see the man behind it? She could see Andi clearly enough, lying face up on the floor while raindrops plopped onto the carpet from the hem of her red trench.

Sera felt her lungs constrict. Fear—no, terror—rushed in.

"You're safe," a soothing male voice intervened. "He can't hurt you this time. Tell me where you are, Sera."

"I'm in Reception. No, I got away. I'm in my office. I'm calling Security. Len answers. I tell him to come, to hurry. Andi's dead. I can still see her face, her eyes. I can hear rain dripping onto the carpet. But in my mind it's not rain, it's blood."

"What about Andi's murderer? Can you see him?"

"I see a coat—maybe a coat. It's khaki, very light. He's wearing a watch, high up on his right forearm. I see his hands and his teeth. He looks wild. He's wearing black latex gloves. I drop the phone and run."

"He can't hurt you, Sera, even if he catches you. You're safe no matter what he does."

"He's strong." Her breath hitched. "Really strong. That's rage mixed with adrenaline. He has a knife. He's going to use it. His coat smells like it's been stored in wet mothballs. This time I miss when I kick him.

"The coat's open, his shirt is torn. I see a tattoo. It's The Shadow. Good masquerading as evil, except with this man it's the other way around.

"He shoves me away, but I can't run. I can't even move, and there's a pain in my head.

Really sharp, like he got me with his knife. I keep seeing Andi's face, and I can still hear the blood—no, the drops of rain—hitting the carpet. Nothing's left after that." Both her voice and her mind hazed. "I'll burn the coat, Andi, promise. I'll never wear red again…"

SURFACING WAS MUCH like waking up from a nightmare, except for some reason she felt oddly peaceful. She still hadn't put a face to the Blindfold Killer, and God knew, all she wanted to do when Hollis eased her back into the now was sleep, but for the first time since it happened, the night made sense. There was a logical sequence of events.

"I left a tiny imprint in your mind." Hollis pushed a steaming mug of hot cocoa into her hands. "Nothing that will harm you or likely last for more than a few days, but perhaps the means to expand upon those things of which you're now aware."

He could have said he'd planted an alien transmitter in her head, and she wouldn't have cared.

When her eyes closed, Hollis, his crowded trailer and even Logan simply dissolved.

She didn't dream about Andi as she'd expected. It was Logan who followed her into sleep. Sexy, mysterious Logan. One of the few men she trusted with her life. The only man she trusted with her heart.

It should have startled her to realize that, but it didn't. It didn't even make her want to run. So she'd rationalize it instead. He'd risked his life more than once to save hers. What woman wouldn't fall just a little bit in love?

Except it wasn't a little bit, and he wasn't open to love. Which might be the only reason she wasn't panicking in her sleep.

Without warning she heard the Blindfold Killer growl. The sound came from below, above and all around her.

Bob Marley played in Andi's office, but it was the steady plop, plop, plop of rain on the carpet that commanded her attention. She hadn't noticed it before.

The killer lurched toward her. His teeth were clenched, but she thought his lips moved. Was he shouting at her?

She picked up snatches of words, something about a graveyard ghoul.

His mouth stopped moving, and he grabbed her. She fought. Although she hadn't before, this time, she freed an arm.

While Bob Marley sang and the raindrops plopped next to Andi's lifeless body, she plowed her fist into his shadowed face.

Chapter Fourteen

Logan avoided the worst of the punch, but she still managed to clip his jaw and a portion of his right cheekbone.

In the darkness behind him, Hollis chuckled. "There's nothing passive about that one, Logan. Having met her, I'm hoping, though likely in vain, that you've set aside what happened back in Los Angeles and are willing to move into a more positive phase of your life."

Logan waited until Sera rolled onto her stomach on Hollis's bed before sliding his friend a dry look. "So the fact that she just tried to deck me says nothing to you, huh?"

"It says she's a fighter, but I deduced that much when she let me take her under against her will."

"She wants her friend's murderer caught. It also pisses her off that people are dying simply because they stand between the killer and her."

"Your uncle for one." Hollis handed him a large mug. "Special blend. Coffee with a kick. I'm sorry about Sig, Logan. He was a good man."

"I know." His eyes slid back to Sera. "He gave her his Sedona rock."

"I see."

Logan wished he did. He made a final check— she was sleeping peacefully now—gave his shoulders a tired roll and drank some of Hollis's coffee.

The concoction burned all the way to his stomach. It would have made his eyes water if he hadn't been prepared.

"Stronger than usual." He sucked air in

through his teeth. "Some reason you think I need it?"

The old man shrugged, smiled, and turned away. "Emotions, floodgates, gut instinct. I went over the short list you sent of the Blindfold Killer's recent victims. My sense is, it's a new set of murders, a new vendetta if you will. You've got a social worker, age fifty-six, a waitress, forty-one, a retired insurance broker, seventy-four and a psychiatrist, twenty-nine. No apparent connection among any of them, and yet under hypnosis, Sera mentioned that a social worker wanted to talk to her."

"Jody Frost." Logan made a long sweep of the clearing through the window. "She's Oakland based. The woman who died worked with troubled kids in San Francisco."

"There still might be a connection."

"It's possible the department didn't go deep enough there. Under hypnosis, Sera said she agreed to meet the Frost woman, but there was nothing on her appointment calendar."

Hollis drained his mug. "Because it wasn't a patient meeting, maybe she left it at a mental note. I did that all the time."

"Yeah, but you're off the wall. Sera isn't."

"I gather you've never heard of her uncle. Dr. Jeffrey Hudson spends five days a week immersed in medical research and development. He's made not strides but leaps in treatment options for more life-threatening conditions than you can name. He runs a clinic and workshops on the side, all pro bono. The man's a complete workaholic. He's also a genius—and you know what they say about genius versus insanity."

"Yeah, I know. Fine line between." Logan's gaze strayed to the bedroom. "She likes cities, Hollis. It's where she belongs and I don't. You'd call us diametrically opposed."

"Would I?" Although the old man's eyes twinkled, he let it go. "Back to your serial killer then. I believe the red tape's key. It could be entirely literal—reference to a system that bogged him down to the point where whatever tether he'd managed to use on his homicidal urges snapped. Or there could be a complex reason. It could also be that each victim added to the strain on that tether. Once unleashed, the monster within went hunting."

"That's comforting."

"Theories only, Logan. I'm sure you have a few of them yourself." He squinted at his novelty owl wall clock. "It's closing on 3:00 a.m., and I'm betting small town living is slowly but surely turning you into a morning man."

Logan glanced at Hollis's bedroom again. "Three o'clock's morning in most people's books. You want to work on our chess game, I'm up for it."

Chuckling, Hollis went in search of the board. "With that lovely lady in there taking up a good three-quarters of your mind, our seven-month-old game will be concluded by dawn. As the potential victor, I have only two small requests." His clear blue eyes met Logan's. "Find the bastard who wants her dead. And if you don't want to marry her, give me the all clear, and I certainly will."

"I LIKE HIM." In the passenger seat of Logan's truck, Sera twirled her hair around one finger. "He's kind, he's clever and he's a better cook than I'll ever be. I still don't like turning my mind over to another person, but at least I don't feel violated. He's a good hypnotist."

"And a crafty chess player." Logan glanced in the rearview mirror. "He wants to marry you."

"Relocate the trailer and I'll think about it." Amused, she surveyed the barely visible strip of road ahead. Rain and murky darkness obliterated everything that wasn't directly in front of them. "You shouldn't have let me sleep for fourteen hours, Logan. Taking into account a two-hour dinner, plus another two hours of hellish driving time, it must be after 9:00 p.m."

He turned the wipers on high as the rain streaming over the windshield came down harder. "We're almost at the highway. Two more hours, and it'll be Flo who's forcing food on you."

Releasing her hair, Sera concentrated on capturing a memory that had been teasing the edges of her brain since she'd woken up.

She spread her fingers out in front of her. "It's like there's a thin layer of smoke between my eyes and his face. All it would take is one good… Whoa." She grabbed the dash when the truck gave two rough, sideways lurches. "Was that a rut?"

"Felt like a trench." Logan shook his head for silence. "I need to hear."

Unless the clatter coming from the rear of the vehicle was normal, Sera suspected a very big problem.

Pulling over, Logan reached into the back for a flashlight. He drew the gun from his waistband and gave it to her along with a quick kiss. "Stay here."

"Logan…" She sighed as the door slammed.

Thankfully, Hollis had insisted she borrow his rain gear. Shoving the door open, she hopped into a puddle.

Even with extra socks, Hollis's boots were far too big. The mud made sucking sounds around her ankles every time she lifted a foot. She wore a hat and an oversized raincoat, but she thought it might be less work simply to get wet. Hindered by rubber and canvas, it took her twice as long as it should have to find Logan.

He was playing his light through the under-carriage when she did. "Pretty sure I told you to stay inside, Sera."

"The last time I did that, I was attacked by a Bulley. I'd rather stick with you." She waited until he drew the light out. "And the verdict is?"

"Cracked axle. We'll have to walk to Moosekill."

The name of the town sounded more daunting than the prospect of slogging through the rain and mud to reach it. She tried to shift a foot and almost left her boot behind. "Is it far?"

"Three or four miles, half of them on the highway."

Bending, she yanked on the stuck boot. "Please tell me there's no danger. You can't believe the Blindfold Killer followed us to Hollis's place, or you wouldn't have taken me there."

Logan scanned the area. "Hollis was a munitions specialist in two wars, and he can still beat the crap out of me in a target shoot. You wouldn't know it by looking, but his trailer's alarmed to the max. He has three dogs you didn't see because he figured they might scare you, and a webcam link with the ax man we saw when we first got there. Even so, the answer to your question is no, I don't think we were followed. At least not all the way." Handing her his flashlight, he opened the driver's door. "Feel better?"

"Tons." Careful to steer clear of the big puddles, she peered through the trees. "What makes you think we were followed at all?"

"Probably the gallon of coffee I drank yesterday."

"Caffeine-induced paranoia's not an answer."

"Cop instinct then. Target leaves town, murderer leaves town. But I'm guessing he's not up for a difficult trek. A few miles on a worse than bad road, chances are he turned back."

"Oh good." She slid her arms through the pack he passed over. "All or partway back?"

"Sixty-four-thousand dollar question, Doc. Can you handle a rifle?"

"Not as well as a gun. Logan." She caught his sleeve as he slung the strap of a badass Winchester over one shoulder. "Are you sure Hollis is safe?"

"I'm sure."

"But us, not so much."

Curling his fingers around her nape, he gave her a kiss that rocked her right down to the toes of Hollis's boots. "I promise he won't hurt you."

Which made her feel better. Until she realized he hadn't made the same promise for himself.

IF THEY'D GONE IN, then they would come out. He said that every time the hatred and fury simmering inside threatened to boil over.

He sat in his stolen vehicle on the edge of the highway. He ate stale donuts, drank cold coffee and listened to country music to stay awake.

He'd get her this time. Her luck couldn't hold forever.

But neither could his. The cop was looking in more than one direction. He was asking more questions, questioning different people. Eventually he'd ask the wrong person and wham, end of charade.

No, he ordered himself, don't think like that. Don't panic. Outmaneuver them. Listen. Learn. Stay one step ahead. It was all about details—and being invisible.

In a controlled movement, he unfolded the white bandanna he always carried and removed the length of red tape hidden inside. When his breath began to heave, he wrapped the tape around his hands and gave it a vicious snap.

He'd blind her and bind her, kiss the nightmare she'd become goodbye and move on to his next victim. Hudson? Problem solved.

Four down, three to go.

SERA NOTICED THAT Logan walked half a pace behind her during the difficult hike to the highway. His pack had to weigh twice as much as hers, and the rifle was no lightweight either. But even with the barrel propped on one shoulder and his eyes in constant motion, he looked like a man out for a nighttime stroll in the woods.

She checked the exasperation that rose when he reached down one-handed to extricate her boot from a mud hole. "How is it that you weigh more than me, and yet I'm the one who keeps getting stuck?"

"You're stepping in the wrong places. Keep to the edge of the path."

"News flash, pal—there hasn't been a path since we veered off that collection of ruts and potholes that no one except the Mantracker would call a road." She breathed out her tension. "You think the Blindfold Killer's waiting for us on the highway, don't you?"

"I think there's a good chance."

"Are you sure your phone can't get a signal?"

"I'll try again when we clear the trees." He steered her around another hole with a gentle nudge on her spine. "You're not going to start complaining, are you?"

"That would be bitchy and pointless." She swatted at a low branch. "I hate bitchiness, and I prefer point-blank to pointless." A moment later, a wet branch slapped her in the face. Shoving it up, she went with her preference. "Why did you leave Los Angeles? You can tell me it's none of my business, but please don't lie and tell me you wanted a change of pace."

"I did."

"Logan."

"There's more to it, but pace factored in."

She glanced at his profile in silhouette. "Is that a polite way of telling me to butt out?"

"No, it's a pragmatic way of saying that here and now might not be the best place for this conversation."

"That response could be construed as avoidance, Chief." But her teasing undertone took the sting out of her words. "Hollis told me he won a long-term chess match against you last night. He also said he thinks you're taking the recent Blindfold Killer murders in a different direction than the San Francisco police. Is that true?"

"All I'm doing is broadening my scope where the murderer's concerned."

"Translated into English that means…"

"I'm leaning toward a copycat."

"Despite the unreleased consistencies in his MO. Why?"

He squinted at a gap in the trees. "Gut feeling, nothing concrete."

"Did I say something under hypnosis?"

"You said quite a lot. I'm still processing most of it." He nodded through the rain. "Highway's up there. I want you to stay back while I check it out. There should be a small filling station and diner just south of here."

She wondered if his mental ruler measured in yards or miles and how, once on the highway, he expected to differentiate between a regular motorist and one with murderous intent.

At least walking would be easier. Except for the ditch they had to wade through and the fact that, in the open, the wind was whipping the rain around in circles.

Lowering the rifle to his side, Logan shrugged off his pack and stepped up onto the pavement. Sera couldn't see any vehicles, but some of the larger boulders looked like they could easily hide one.

She forced herself not to follow him up. If the murderer was waiting, he wouldn't hesitate to take Logan out. He'd probably take anyone at this point.

Something rocketed out of the bushes behind her. Swinging around, she snapped her gun up, and for an instant, stopped breathing.

She'd seen him. As the rabbit she'd startled had darted out of the underbrush, the killer's face had blinked on and off in her head.

He'd been lunging at her, his mouth moving, the fingers of his gloved left hand outstretched, a bloody knife clutched in his right. Had he been calling her a ghoul as he ran?

"Come on," she urged her resistant brain. "Let me see him again. Just for another half second. That's all I need."

"Sera."

She cut off most of the gasp as a hand came down on her shoulder. She couldn't stop her other reaction, which was to jerk free and spin. And thankfully recognize before she fired.

Logan regarded the gun lodged against his rib cage. "I know the wind's loud, but I did call your name three times before I actually touched you."

She dropped her head onto his chest. "I saw his face. Just for a moment, but there was no smoke or shadows this time. Then, blink, it went dark."

"Nothing stood out?"

She looked up. "Sorry. I wasn't expecting a breakthrough. A rabbit caught me off guard. Suddenly he was there. Then he wasn't. Next time, I won't let it go." She waved the tip of her gun toward the road. "Anything?"

"Nothing and no one." His lips twitched. "That I could see."

She gave him a kiss. "I love a positive man. Shall we go?"

For an answer, he held out a hand.

The highway consisted of two thin lanes with pitted shoulders and no lights. Which meant Sera could see about two feet in front of her at any given time. Still, walking was a piece of cake by comparison, and Logan's presence, coupled with the promise of a twenty-four-hour filling station, lifted her spirits to the point where her nerves only went zing every few seconds.

"It must be hell to be part of a witness protection program," she remarked above the whip and whirl of the wind. "Anyone you know ever done that?"

"One or two."

"Do you know where they are?"

"Yeah." His eyes combed the darkness. "They're dead."

"Ah." New topic, she decided. "How long were you…?"

He didn't need to silence her. Sera did it herself as a pair of headlights careened into view around a sharp bend. Something about the movement of the vehicle set her nerves on alert. She swore she heard tires squeal above the rush of rain and wind.

"Get down."

Not waiting, Logan tossed her across the ditch into a patch of prickly bushes.

What sounded like a truck minus its muffler roared closer. For a moment, Sera thought the driver might simply be a joyriding teenager. Then the back end fishtailed, and the entire vehicle swung out. Skidding sideways on the wet pavement, it screeched to a halt in front of them.

For a moment, there was nothing except the growl of the truck's engine. Steaming headlights cut through the gloom.

In the bushes, Sera choked back a scream when a hand gripped her ankle.

"Get behind a tree," Logan told her.

She struggled to separate Hollis's raincoat from the thorns poking through it. "Can you see him?"

"Not yet. Tree, Sera."

Finally, the prickles released her. She located the nearest pine and crawled toward it, skirting the base until the trunk stood between her and the truck.

A second later, two bullets winged the outer edge and sent strips of bark flying.

She spied the vague outline of the driver, but of course Logan was gone. Lamont Cranston had nothing on the Blue Ridge police chief.

More shots grazed the bark. Sera counted to

bolster herself, then brought her arms up and fired at the killer's outline. She knew by the sound that she struck metal.

To her left, Logan used his rifle. He blew out one of the headlights and possibly the right front tire.

A spray of bullets peppered the air. She heard feet sloshing through the ditch and up the other side. She thought she glimpsed two guns in the man's hands, but she couldn't be sure. Squeezing off three more shots, she prepared to run.

Logan snared her by the waist before she could move. "Other direction," he said and motioned northward.

"But we can't get help that way."

"Shhh."

Although she wanted to protest, Sera clamped her mouth shut and did as he said—as quietly as she could.

The wind whistled around them. Rain pellets stung her cheeks. She had no idea where the Blindfold Killer was. Ahead, behind, in the ditch tracking them.

"Stay low," Logan cautioned.

Like she could stand with his hand pressed to her neck.

The bushes thickened. "Stop." He said it so softly she almost didn't hear him. "Don't move."

Ten seconds ticked by. Twenty. "Where is he?" she whispered.

"Not sure. Hiding, rethinking." Logan's eyes skimmed the overgrown bramble. "He's not a hunter."

Sera supposed that was a point in their favor, but lucky shots happened, especially when the aggressor carried two high-powered weapons.

A branch cracked close by. Shoving her behind him, Logan shouldered his rifle and fired. A howl like an enraged bull erupted but was swiftly silenced.

"Was that him?"

"Yes. Go." He gave her a push. "Make your way back to the road."

"What are you going to do?"

"Keep him busy. Take the gun. Use it if you see him."

"But…"

"Do it, Sera. Get as close to the road as you can, but keep out of sight."

Arguing would be a waste of time and an unneeded distraction so she swallowed her objections and started off.

The black strip of highway seemed miles away. She eased down into the ditch and up the other side. Logan must have a plan. Unless he was just Marshal Dillon squaring off against a particularly nasty villain.

She was crawling through soggy vegetation when a fresh round of bullets blasted through the air over her head. She thought about firing back, but the sound of rifle shot kept her moving forward.

Far ahead on the road, she spotted a glimmer of light. And another. Her heart jumped into her throat. Someone was coming.

Bullets continued to whiz above her. She couldn't stand and wasn't sure she should. If the unsuspecting driver slowed, the Blindfold Killer might switch targets and another innocent person could die.

Logan got off three more shots. Breath held, Sera waited for the murderer's reply. But there were no more bullets, and, as if a curtain had lifted in her mind, she realized why.

Not only were there headlights on the approaching vehicle, but also the familiar red and blue flashers of a police car.

The cavalry had arrived.

Chapter Fifteen

"Sorry I didn't pursue him, Logan, but you said you were near Willie's Bog, so I stopped when I saw you. You're lucky you got a message through to the station from there. Nine times out of ten, all you get's dead air."

The Moosekill police chief handed Sera a towel to wipe the mud from her hands and face.

"I'm gonna guess that at this particular moment, neither of you cares about what-ifs or apologies. Still, I'll spread the word and send someone out to tow your truck." He indicated a blurry log structure nestled among a heavy stand of trees. "Moosekill Lodge, dead ahead.

It'll be full up, but the owner usually leaves one room free for emergencies. I figure this qualifies."

A naturally chatty man, he didn't seem to require any responses. He pulled up outside the lodge, had a word with the manager and, while Logan talked to Fred on his cell, returned dangling a key for Sera who was in the process of shedding her sodden gear.

"You're good to go in the executive suite. Car dealer from Billings is booked for the day after tomorrow, but until then, the manager says enjoy."

Replacing Hollis's boots and socks with a pair of wedge-heeled sandals, Sera thanked him. She made a detour to the washroom, then handed her dripping outerwear to a woman in a leather vest and hat who promised to have it dried out by morning.

Ten minutes later, the manager ushered them into the third floor corner suite. He turned two lamps on low and told them to make full use of the facilities, which included a hot tub and a mini bar. Winking broadly at Logan, he tipped his hat and left.

Logan tossed his backpack, hat and wet coat aside while Sera checked out the simple but pleasing decor. "You thought there'd be animal heads on the walls, didn't you?" he asked.

"Maybe." A large fruit basket sat on the bar. "I like the watercolors better. How come I got valet service, and you didn't?"

"You probably look like you expect it, and I don't."

"There's that snob thing again." A package of dates caught her eye. "Is there a restaurant here?"

"Two, and room service."

She hit a button on the remote and searched until she found the Eagles. Giving her damp hair a shake, she bit into a date. She turned to offer the other half to Logan, then spied a streak of blood on his left arm and choked.

"What?" He frowned when she strode over to

tug at the front of his shirt. "Not that I mind, but why are you undressing me?"

Changing tactics, she yanked his sleeve up and made a sound of exasperated disbelief. "You might have mentioned that you'd been shot."

He looked down, still frowning. "That? That's a graze. Shot involves an ambulance, a hospital and occasionally a blood transfusion."

"If you don't know it, Logan, infections are frighteningly easy to come by."

"Are you always this dramatic?"

"Are you always this pigheaded?"

He trapped her wrist before she could probe further. "Trust me. I've had worse."

"Oh, I'm sure of it." She batted his hand away. "Now you can be a good cop and let me look, or I can sedate you and force compliance. Your choice."

"You weren't upset when you punched me last night."

"I punched… Really?" She thought back. "I don't remember that."

"I think I took one for the Blindfold Killer."

Momentarily sidetracked, she touched a finger to the faint mark on his jaw. "That was me?"

"You have a mean right hook, Doc."

Reluctant humor bubbled up. "Bear that in mind when I tell you that you could use a few stitches. However, seeing as you saved my life, I'll let you off with antiseptic, gauze and a single shot of whiskey from the mini-bar."

"Sounds like a deal." Locking his eyes on hers, Logan fingered the narrow strap of her silk top. "Tell me, do you ever not dress to seduce?"

A tremor shimmered through her. "Are you trying to distract me?"

"Not particularly. I already avoided the needle."

"Uh-huh." She hooked a finger in the front of his shirt. "So having shied away from your deepest fear, you're thinking mission accomplished, is that it?"

"Not exactly." Either they were moving, or the

walls were closing in. "What I'm thinking is that a bandage can probably wait."

"Because life is short and I'm wearing a sexy top?"

"That works as a starting point."

So did the lamplight that pooled like silver on the dark wood floor. Around them, the Eagles sang about dreamers and signs and taking things to their limit.

At that moment, Sera felt there were no limits or barriers anywhere. Desire spiked through reason and created a jumble of sensations in her body and mind.

Logan kept his eyes fastened on hers. "You should run, Doc. Or at least slap a hand to my chest and tell me to back off."

Setting both hands on his chest, she let them slide upward until her fingers tangled in his hair. "Why is that, exactly?"

"Because having sex will complicate the hell out of both our lives."

Laughter sparkled in her eyes. "Nothing about

my life has ever been anything less than com-plicated, Logan." Letting temptation win, she gave his lip a tantalizing bite and at the same time rolled her body against him. "I've dreamed about doing that too many times to count."

"Only that?"

She bumped him hip to hip. "What do you think?"

"That some of the things I've imagined during more than one sleepless night might actually happen."

When his mouth covered hers, every part of her responded. It was like she'd been zapped with a thousand volts of silken electricity.

Careful not to touch his wounded arm, she ran her hands from his shoulders to his wrists and held. She wanted the bed under her and Logan on top. She wanted to feel him fully aroused with the barrier of their clothing still between them. Then piece by piece, she wanted those layers gone, until they were skin to skin, heat pouring into heat. Until they both sizzled and burned.

Using her hold on him against her, he hauled her forward, then drew back so his mouth was a mere inch from hers. "Last chance for that slap, Sera."

She heard the words, but only in a distant, foggy part of her brain. The second his mouth came back onto hers, every thought, every scrap of reason simply vanished.

His tongue plunged in, hot and hungry. She met it with a greed that intrigued her.

Pressed against him, she felt his muscles tense. Her fingers slid up under his shirt to explore the sleek, smooth skin of his back.

She didn't want to stop kissing him. His tongue was sparking incredible sensations in her body. Pinpoints of light glittered behind her eyelids, but in the end, it all came down to taste and touch and wanting him inside her.

With an impatient sound, she brought her hands around to the button of his jeans. The stubble on his jaw scraped her cheek as he kissed her face and throat. She nipped the corners of his mouth, then gasped out a laugh when they landed on the mattress.

Raising her arms above her head, she let him dispose of her slithery top. Her lace bra followed. A shiver raced across her skin. Recognizing it for what it was—pure desire—she shifted her hips.

Her crop pants vanished. So did her lace thong. She pushed his jeans away, then, kneeling to face him, ran her palms over his torso and lower, until she reached the hot, hard length of him.

With a cryptic half smile and a smoldering look in his eyes, Logan cupped her face and took possession of her mouth again. When he drew away, she let her head fall back. And hissed in a breath of shock and pleasure as his tongue circled her breast.

Desire surged from nipple to thigh, each spike driving deeper than the one before. When he raised his head, she took the lead, capturing his mouth and pushing him onto the mattress.

A smile stole across her lips as she got her first full look at his naked body. Straddling him, she moved her hips in a slow, sensuous motion.

A moment later she was flat on her back with no idea how she'd gotten there.

He went up on one elbow just far enough to stare into her eyes. "I knew you were a damn witch the first time I saw you."

She took him in her hands again. "Flattery won't get you out of this, Chief."

His features shadowed, he lowered his mouth to hers. "So who wants out?"

Those were the last words Sera heard. When his fingers plunged inside her, her head arched on the pillow. She bucked against him. Her nails dug into his hips and the world crumbled to dust.

She felt herself racing upward, desperate to discover that place only Logan could take her.

A shudder of release rocked her from the

inside out. Heat flared. She knew she said his name, wondered hazily if she screamed it, as he took her up and up and up.

Heat streaked through her veins. When she wrapped her legs around him, his muscles, already straining, went rigid. Eyes open, she brought him inside.

Together they rolled until she was on top and he was holding her, pumping himself into her.

Her body bowed back, absorbing each long, hard thrust. Color and sound collided. Sensation swept through her. For an instant, the world went absolutely still, then burst apart in a shower of sparks that had her crying out as she spiraled into the fiery center.

He might have said something. She couldn't hear over the throb of blood in her head. She knew he caught her before her muscles gave out and she toppled from the bed.

"Stay with me, Sera," he murmured.

Still inside her, he brought her lower, until her hair fell on either side of his face. He kissed her cheeks, then her mouth and finally, easing her down beside him, pressed his forehead to hers.

She skimmed wondering fingers across his shoulder. "If I can feel you, I must still be alive." Sliding her leg over his, she nuzzled the bruise on his jaw. "Pretty sure you are, too."

"Don't count on it." He closed his eyes and breathed out. "We're slow to die in my family."

She had just enough strength to laugh. "You've got a family?"

"Yeah. Of vipers."

Touching a finger to his lower lip, she pressed down, kissed the imprint. "That was amazing, Logan."

"No, that was great."

"Excuse me?"

His eyes gleamed in the wash of watery light. "Night's young, Sera. I'm betting we can take it from great to way past amazing by morning."

With her humor and some portion of her strength restored, she pushed him onto his back. "You're on, cowboy." She kissed him hard and deep, felt him stir inside her and grinned. "I hope you're up for a very long ride."

THERE WAS NO room service available at 2:00 a.m., so they ate dates and black olives in the hot tub. Afterward, dripping and ravenous, they made love again.

The wind died. The clouds broke apart. The rain turned to mist and for a heartbeat of time, the horror that was the Blindfold Killer disappeared.

Later, on the floor, with Logan's hat on her head and wearing the cop shirt from his pack, Sera poured them both a glass of California red.

Their room overlooked a small lake surrounded by woods. Now that the clouds had dispersed, stars sparkled on the water, bouncing back diamond points of light. An almost dizzying number of them, she thought and turned her eyes, shielded by the brim of Logan's hat, to the man who was and had been for some time, the main source of her curiosity.

"Is your arm okay?" She glanced at the make-shift bandage she'd fashioned after their second blistering round of sex.

He sat with his back against the sofa, facing both her and the window. "It never wasn't, Sera." A smile touched his lips. "But as a physician you won't believe that, so yeah, it's fine, and thanks for killing what little pain there was."

She set the wine bottle aside. "Why am I sensing a mood? You were amiable enough a few minutes ago."

"Conversation's not necessary when you're making love. Heart rate slows, sanity returns, and I know what's coming."

She chose to be nice and moved from a sexy curl to a cross-legged position on the carpet. "You don't have to tell me anything you don't want to, Logan. I don't like being pushed either. I only asked you about L.A. earlier because I was feeling cranky."

Balancing his glass on a single raised knee, he

regarded the contents half-lidded. "I was born in northern Montana, in a town called Sorley, population six hundred and twelve. My parents were churchgoing Baptists. Every Sunday, my father asked for forgiveness for beating the crap out of my brothers and me. Seven brothers," he added with more of a smile than Sera would have expected. "Six were older, one was younger. My mother raised chickens, canned garden vegetables and prayed for all our souls.

"One by one, we got out. Four of us wound up on the West Coast. One joined the Marines, one became a cop, two went into business for themselves."

Sera knew by his tone that "business" was merely a euphemism for… "Drugs?" she assumed, watching what little she could see of his face.

"Pretty much. Might have been some other illegals thrown in from time to time, but mostly they stuck to what they knew."

She touched his ankle. "You don't have to do this, Logan."

"Hollis thinks I do." He raised his glass, drank. "And you're curious."

"Not at the cost of… Okay, yes," she admitted, "I'm curious."

"So I'll give you the short version and satisfy both of us. Ethan was the real bad ass. He hated me for being a cop. I met a woman, Sherry, also a cop. We got involved, worked out a routine, worked ourselves into a rut. Things got rocky, but that's how it is for cops. Relationship deteriorated. Then, one night, she got shot."

"Oh, damn. Logan, you really don't…"

"Sherry didn't die, but the guy who shot her did. Dead man's name was Spider. Spider shot Sherry, Ethan shot Spider. I discovered that Ethan and Sherry were lovers and had been for months. She knew what he was, but being what she was, she turned a blind eye. Until—wrong place, wrong time. One of Ethan's cronies tried to take her out. Now my brother's in prison for murder, and Sherry, who was dismissed from the department, is doing the books for a small chain of movie theaters in Nebraska. I stayed in L.A. for a while, then decided to hell with it. Sympathy sucked. Clean break worked better. I headed north to see Hollis, got sidetracked, got a new life."

"Got a life you like," she corrected. "Maybe the life you should have had from the start."

"That would depend on your view of fate. Fred thinks it was meant to be. I say detours happen. Sometimes they're good, sometimes not. The trick is to keep things simple, don't get attached."

"So you can take Blue Ridge or leave it?"

"Leave it in the lurch, no. But knowing the job's been competently filled, yeah, I could walk."

"Uh-huh." When he arched a brow at her tone, she set her glass aside and got to her knees. "Still a shrink, Chief." She batted his bent leg until he straightened it, then, kneeling over his lap, played with the dusting of dark hair on his chest. "As a shrink, I'll say that psychoanalysis has its place, and this isn't it. So I'll go with my feminine intuition and speculate that if you hadn't liked where you ended up, you'd have taken off two plus years ago. I'll also add that you're not the only person in this room who's chosen the wrong lover. I almost got engaged to a man three years ago who insisted I was the woman of his dreams."

"Which made him wrong because?"

"Oh, his claim might have been true, except in his fantasy, he married the woman he loved, then had sex with—well, pretty much any other woman who caught his eye. Like I said, Logan—my life, very complicated."

When he shifted her to a more telling part of his lap, she grinned. "Does this mean we're good?"

His eyes began to gleam as he gripped her hips. "Good's never been the problem, Sera.

In fact, right now, I'm not sure what the problem is."

"In that case, let me fill you in." Pushing his hat back, Sera lowered her mouth until it was only a whisper away from his. "From my perspective, it's a problem of time, distance and should we try for the bed? Or say damn the consequences, and make love right here on the floor?"

OUCH, OUCH, DAMMIT, ouch!

He had to twist the red tape tightly around his thigh where the bastard police chief's bullet had gone in. Thankfully, it had also come out. But he'd lost both blood and a golden opportunity because of it.

He'd had to change a flat tire in the rain, fight through the dizziness that had threatened to swamp him and in the end spend another night in his stolen truck.

He toughed it out on a side road between where he'd been and where he needed to be.

Sweat beaded on his forehead and upper lip. His thigh was on fire, and he was having monstrous dreams.

He heard his mother scratching at the door. She wanted to come back. Papa said okay, but this time she had to stay.

She did—for a month. Then she left again, and Papa's heart, already half broken, crumbled to pieces.

"It's you and me now, son. Just us, no one else…"

Time rolled on. Years became decades.

"No one else," Papa insisted. "Just you and me…"

"Just us," the killer agreed in his sleep.

That's how it had been—until it hadn't.

That's when he'd gotten mad.

Eleven dead, murdered by the Blindfold Killer. Suspect arrested. Released. But the cops kept tabs on him. For a while.

Released suspect vanished. Did the dumb cops find him? Not so far. Maybe not ever.

The rain drumming on the roof of his truck slowed and finally stopped. The fire in his thigh made his leg go numb.

Maybe he'd die because of the Blue Ridge police chief. Maybe he'd never reach his goal of seven dead. But he'd get Sera Hudson. One way or another, he'd take her out.

Papa would give him a hero's welcome.

Chapter Sixteen

"This isn't exactly how I envisioned our morning going, Logan." Sera waved at the cloud of mosquitoes that swarmed out of the weeds around her. "I figured at 7:00 a.m. we'd be eating, not be eaten for, breakfast. Won't the rain have washed away any blood the Blindfold Killer lost? Assuming you shot him and that howl we heard last night wasn't him breaking an ankle in this rat hole of a ditch."

Crouching, Logan separated a wet patch of crab grass and thistles. "Answer to that long-winded question is possibly, but it's still worth a look."

Because he was right, and Fred wouldn't arrive to pick them up for an hour in any case, she squelched past him in Hollis's boots, shielded her eyes and endeavored to recreate the scene.

Last night's rain was nothing but a memory at this point. The sky was blue, the road was dry and the temperature had already climbed past eighty degrees.

Pivoting, she located the tree she'd used for cover, then slapped at a persistent deer fly. "I think we were twenty or thirty yards to the right of this spot."

"You were." He shifted a heavy tangle of vines. "I was moving toward him."

Something glinted ahead of her. Bending, Sera sloshed over to check it out.

Through the tall blades of grass, she spotted a gray metal cylinder. "I found a bullet casing," she called to Logan.

"Gun or rifle?"

She raised her voice. "Rifle, I think."

He waded over bare-chested, oblivious to the teeming insect life. "It's one of mine." Then he took another step and reached out to shift a thistle.

"What?"

With his free hand, he pulled her down next to him. "Blood," he said. She saw the gleam in his eyes. "And I'm betting it isn't mine."

BETH RUSHED OUT of the clinic the moment Logan and Sera braked at the police station in Fred's four by four.

"People have been asking for you since you left town. I thought you'd be back yesterday so I've been taking appointments. We're booked solid today." She popped her head around Sera to beam at Logan. "Morning, Chief. Toby's got Edgar Bulley waiting in your office. Trouble with your truck?"

"It's a long story," Logan told her. He glanced at the clinic and saw a lot of movement inside. "Looks like you'll have your hands full today,

Doc. I'll send Toby over to keep an eye on things."

The look she slanted him had guilt twisting in his belly, but he was used to that. Shutting it down, he left her to deal with Beth and a raft of expectant patients alone.

Although he hadn't told her everything about his life last night, he'd said enough. Too much by his standards and with too little urging.

"Chief, hi. Thank God you're back." Stressed to the point where his hair stuck up, Toby vaulted to his feet. "Old Edgar's in your office. He wants the rest of his grandsons released, says stuff's going on at the farm and there's only three there to keep watch. He might be telling the truth because some of the site workers who are camped in that field Abe leased from him say they've heard buckshot in the ravine. Plus we've had a bunch of small thefts and burglaries lately."

"I know. I'll talk to him." Logan took a last look at Sera, then turned his attention to his young deputy. "I have to drive down to Casper this morning. I want you to stay at the clinic until Fred gets back from Moosekill with my truck. Make sure the back and side doors are double locked and Beth goes into the examining room with every patient. Send Annabelle out to my place to get Ella, and tell Walter to take a drive around the resort site, see if he can locate Wayne Postle."

"The biker guy you ticketed? Is he still here?"

"Sera and I saw him on our way in. He was heading north."

"Got it." Toby kept a pencil poised above his notepad. "Anything else?"

Logan glanced at the florist's shop on the corner but shook his head. "No, that's it."

Hostile voices emerging from the cells had his deputy edging toward the door. "I hope you got lots of rest in Moosekill, Logan. Lester's on a tear, and you know what Victor and Lloyd get like."

"Yeah, I know. Don't worry, Toby, they'll be free by sundown."

"Uh, are you sure that's—well, I guess you know what you're doing."

With the Bulleys, yes. With any other part of his life, not at all. Except for one thing, he thought, moving his grazed arm. He had a bullet casing and two samples of blood for the lab in Casper. If Hugh Paxton was behind the recent killings, he'd know about it by tomorrow. If not—well, one way or another he'd get the person who was.

And decide when he had him whether the guy was going in alive.

OKAY, SO NOW he was going to avoid her. Sera thought she could have scripted this part.

Night falls, make love. Stars and wine come out, talk, make love again. Sun rises, reality hits, dive back into the investigation. Stay there, focus, until what's familiar reappears. Then, big sigh, duck out.

If she hadn't been so busy, she would have been annoyed. She might even have confronted him. But patient after patient filed into the clinic, so many of them that the waiting room was never anything short of SRO.

Toby brought Ella over within half an hour of her arrival. The young deputy settled into a folding chair while Ella made herself at home between examining rooms. Beth created new files, kept track of names and made appointments for return visits.

Benny, the first Bulley she'd met, limped in after lunch with several nasty lacerations above his right ankle.

"What?" He fixed her with a bloodshot glare. "Stepped in a rabbit trap is all. Nothing illegal about trapping varmints."

Sera examined the bruised and bloody wounds. "Must have been some big rabbit you were looking to trap, Benny. When did this happen?"

He had trouble climbing onto the table, which

was no wonder—he smelled like a distillery. "Only been out of jail for two days," he muttered, then caught sight of an anatomical diagram and shuddered. "Guess it was the first night."

"So you were just wandering aimlessly in the dark."

"I grew up on that farm. I could wander around blindfolded and not get lost."

"Is that why you stepped in a trap? Because you were wearing a blindfold?"

He flung an arm out. "I stepped in the frigging trap 'cause someone moved it. My brother set 'em one place, and suddenly they were some place else."

"Some place far away?"

"Far enough. Are you gonna make it so my foot doesn't turn green and have to be sawed off or not?"

"Would you feel anything if I did saw it off?"

He jerked back so fast, he almost pitched off the table. "You're as crazy as Prichard."

"Not crazy, Benny, observant. Swing yourself around and put your leg up so I can do a more thorough examination."

"No saws, right?"

"Do you see any saws?" she asked patiently.

Clearly mistrustful, he did as she instructed. "I don't want no vitamin shot either," he warned.

"Tetanus, yes. Vitamin, no."

"Right." He scowled. "What's tetanus?"

"Lockjaw," she said cheerfully. "Extremely unpleasant, sometimes even fatal. Don't worry, though. You're young and healthy, and I'm a whiz with needles. If you're squeamish, we can keep talking, take your mind off what I'm doing."

Noticeably less belligerent, he gave a hesitant nod. "Yeah, we can talk… About what?"

Smiling, she tore the leg of his filthy pants and watched him go from pale to pasty. "Why don't you start by telling me where the trap you stepped in was supposed to be and who you think might have moved it?"

DAMN THE WOMAN, Logan thought in irritation. She haunted him all the way to Casper and back. She was still in his head at four o'clock when Fred returned from Montana with his truck.

"You'll be riding on a used right rear axle stripped from a Dodge that's been sitting in some geezer's barn for the last two years." The big man swiped a layer of sweat from his forehead. "It was either that or order a new one, and I didn't figure you'd want to wait three days." He wrinkled his nose and sniffed. "Thought old Edgar wanted his grandsons released."

Perched on one of the front office desks, Logan perused a clipboard. "When old Edgar becomes chief of police, he can put revolving doors on the cells. Until then, it's my call."

Victor Bulley rattled his cell door. "You're not playing fair, Logan. You put Lester in here after Lloyd and me, but you let him out before. He's the one pulled a knife on the doc, not us."

Without raising his head, Logan called back.

"We found a wad of cash under the floorboard of your truck, not Lester's."

"Lester trusts banks, I don't."

"Yeah? Thing is, Victor, I don't trust you."

He heard voices and knew the two remaining Bulleys were arguing. With a glance at Fred, he grinned. "Something you want to tell me, Lloyd?"

"No," Victor bellowed.

"Yes," his brother snapped.

Another squabble erupted, prompting Fred to shake his head. "How old are they now?"

Logan watched a man with curly brown hair and a cloth pressed to his cheek go into the clinic. He also saw a lot of bunting and banners that hadn't been there when he and Sera had left for Montana.

Blue Ridge Days had arrived. The bleachers would go up tonight, the booths and signs tomorrow. Tourist numbers, already increased, would double by Thursday for the three-day celebration. Add in a carnival, food tents, detours all around Main Street, and you had one big headache waiting to happen.

Back in the cells, Victor finally exploded. "Oh for crap's sake, Logan, you win. Guy paid us to start something in Tommy Gray Wolf's bar the other night. Said we should go for the pretty doc because you'd be on us like a buzzard on a carcass."

Logan returned his attention to the clipboard. "Give me a name."

"Didn't get one."

"A description then."

"Don't have one." When Logan didn't respond, the big Bulley heaved out a breath. "Look, he kept to the shadows, okay? Stood there, said his piece, paid up, took off."

"And stunk like Aunt Linda's hope chest," Lloyd shouted. "You met Aunt Linda, Logan. She lives in our…"

"I know where she lives." Standing, he motioned Fred to the front window and headed for the cells. Resting a shoulder on the corner, he said, "Keep talking."

Lloyd made a jerky motion. "Nothing else to tell. Money's money. We took it and—well, I s'pose I got kinda curious at that. Asked him did he know the doc from somewhere."

Logan nudged his hat forward. "And he replied...?"

"Didn't at first. But when he started to go, I heard him say she was a detail he'd screwed up. Said he shoulda known better than to judge a book by its cover."

SERA WAS MAKING notes and Beth was on the phone when a man came in holding a wad of cotton to his cheek.

"Got sprayed with a bunch of sparks and cinders while I was wiring the resort kitchen." He grimaced. "Some of the cinders stuck."

"That's gotta sting." Sera set the chart aside. "Come on, I'll take a look."

"Wait, Doctor." Beth covered the mouthpiece. "Sue, our midwife's got a breech baby trying to be born, a big one. She wants you to come because there's a lot of blood, and it's a long ambulance ride to Casper."

Blanching, the man with the cinders waved her away. "Don't worry about me. See to the baby."

Reaching for her medical bag, Sera gave the contents a quick check. "Have I met you?" she asked him.

He managed a grin. "Not yet, but I saw you out at Frank's Diner a few nights ago. Reckon I'll see you once or twice more as the work gets sparkier."

Beth wrote down an address and stabbed the paper at Toby. "You get the doc to Green Street lickety split, or my granddaughter's picnic basket will be off-limits to you at the auction this weekend."

What did she know about breech babies? Sera wondered. In the real world, what did she know about delivering babies at all?

Time for an emergency phone call.

She used her speed dial while they wound their way through the streets of town. "Be home, be home, be home," she pleaded under her breath.

For a minute, she thought she was going to get her uncle's voice mail, but he picked up at the last second.

"Hi, Uncle Jeffrey." Not wanting to shake an already-nervous Toby's faith, she twisted in her seat and lowered her voice. "No, I'm fine. I need a quick refresher on breech babies." She glanced out the windshield. "I can't remember if..."

A disbelieving double take stopped the question cold. "Toby, look out!" she shouted and barely had time to brace as a battered blue truck shot down the center of the sloped street.

The driver was speeding and weaving and, by the time he straightened the vehicle out, heading straight for them.

A DOMESTIC DISTURBANCE call that came in after five o'clock put Logan and his deputy Annabelle a mile from the station when the crash occurred. His two-way went off while he was muscling a hotheaded Bulley cousin into his truck.

"What was that sound?" he asked Fred on the other end.

"I hate to think. I'm on my way to Fourth and Spencer Hill."

"Is Toby still with Sera?"

"He is, but they left so the doc could help deliver a baby. I was giving a juvenile shoplifter a stern warning, or I'd've been on their tail."

Fear wrenched in Logan's stomach. "I'll be there in five." He shoved the sulking cousin in Annabelle's direction. "Take this one, too. Front seat, backseat. Any more trouble, JT, you're in for a week."

"She started it." The man glared at his wife who twitched a tattooed shoulder at him.

With one last shove, Logan left Annabelle to deal.

It took him less than four minutes to reach

Spencer Hill. What he saw sent ice water spurting through his veins.

The back end of Toby's truck was impossibly wedged between two large trees. Across the street, resting on its crumpled roof, an ancient blue Ford rocked back and forth as its angry driver rattled the undercarriage.

Logan spared him a look—he didn't appear to be injured—dismissed the stream of questions being hurled at him by several excited bystanders and located Toby at the curb.

"What happened?" He spotted Fred and motioned him toward the driver of the battered Ford. "Where's Sera?"

"Guy's brakes failed. No one was hurt, so Sera went on to Green Street. I didn't know if I should go with her or not, but I figured not. It's only a short drive, and I made her take Ella. I tried to call it in, but my truck's a mess, my cell phone won't work and I lost my two-way."

Logan looked at Fred, who gave him a thumbs up. "What's the address, and who drove her?"

"One-seven-one Green. My minister took her, so I know she's okay."

She might be okay, Logan thought, but he'd be a mess until sometime next week.

His cell phone rang as he turned back toward the gathering crowd. Mildly annoyed, he unhooked it. "Logan."

"It's a girl," Jenny-Lynn sang. "Doc Sera and Sue were awesome. They got her turned, and she popped right out, pink and healthy."

"Glad to hear it. Who's with you?"

"Nadine and Jessie-Lynn. Proud papa's on the front porch with his head between his knees."

Logan relaxed. He told Jenny-Lynn he'd be there in half an hour and ended the call.

"What do you think?" Fred dogged Logan around the flipped Ford. "Could someone have rigged this to happen?"

"In a paranoid world, yes. In the real one..." He crouched for a better view. "Lot of vehicles breaking down lately."

He stood. "Toby, has Walter rounded up that out-of-town biker yet?"

The young deputy joined them, shaking his broken phone. "Last I heard, no, and the guy hasn't showed up at the work site lately, so Abe's not happy."

Fred poked his shoulder. "Don't forget, Logan, the guy was shooting beer cans off one of Edgar Bulley's fences last week."

"I haven't forgotten."

"He's also got a record."

"And a confirmed ID."

"I still don't trust him. He's up to something, and two'll get you ten it isn't good. Any ideas what it might be?"

"One or two." But nothing he intended to share. His cell phone beeped as a pair of calls came in simultaneously.

Regarding the screen, he smiled. "Get to Green Street, Fred. Toby, with me." Zinging nerves were replaced by a surge of adrenaline. "Your cousins are using their knives again."

ENERGIZED AFTER THE birth of a healthy baby girl, Sera returned to the clinic. She dispatched her last patient at 8:45, sent a frazzled Beth on her way and, leaving Fred in the waiting room with a fast-food order, straightened up the second examining room. She refused to think about Logan any more. She'd been doing it for most of the day and hadn't gotten anywhere.

So, naturally, when her cell phone rang, it was his name that appeared on-screen.

The best-laid plans, she reflected and pressed Talk. "I'm fine, Chief. Closing up shop and still pumped."

"Congratulations. Any memory breaks?"

"I wish." She locked the medicine cabinet, dimmed the lights and released her hair. "Whatever it was Hollis planted in my head, it hasn't kicked in yet. Except I keep humming Bob Marley, and I'm visualizing a forearm now with a tan line on it instead of a scratched chrome watch. Go figure."

"Would a late dinner help?"

Despite the lazy drawl, Sera sensed he was revved. "Are we talking payback here?"

"Not unless you'll settle for take-out pizza on the ridge."

Curiouser and curiouser. "Should I wear sneakers for this mysterious outing?"

"Might be an idea."

She sighed. "You're such a puzzle, Logan. You don't like anchovies, do you?"

"Hate 'em. We'll stop by the house so you can change. Ten minutes?"

"No problem." Hoisting the strap of her medical bag over one bare shoulder, Sera turned the radio off, dug her iPod out and popped her earbuds in.

From the waiting room, Fred mimed that he was going to the washroom.

Sera nodded. Head bent, she scanned for U2. Then froze when the dead bolt on the alley door snapped back and the knob began to turn.

Chapter Seventeen

"I swear, Logan, I thought I was looking at a Victorian undertaker—tall, hollow-cheeked and quietly furious with me for invading his medical space." Sera shivered off the unpleasant recollection. "By the way, your office and the mayor's are going to hear about this, so fair warning there. Doctor Rufus Prichard is supremely pissed off and looking to kick my butt out of town, right before he mounts his high horse and rides snottily into the sunset."

"Leaving us one physician and a jackass down." After parking his truck near the top of Blue Ridge, Logan pulled out a backpack and a large flat box. "Pizza's thermal wrapped—in case we get sidetracked."

Sera slid her arms into a black cotton shirt to combat the night insects. She'd gone with designer hiking boots and jeans, a ball cap and a ponytail. Who said urban and country couldn't meet in the middle?

"Are we planning to get sidetracked?" she asked as they undertook the remainder of the climb on foot.

He smiled a little. "It could happen."

"That's an intriguing answer. Will I enjoy this side venture?"

"You might—if I'm right and Flo and Fred are out of the frame by the time we get back."

"Or Doc Prichard isn't waiting in ambush on your back porch."

"He's not that energetic."

"Maybe he needs a vitamin shot." Planting her hands on her hips, she sized up the rock ledge in front of her. "Logan, why aren't we using flashlights? Please tell me we're not setting a trap for the Blindfold Killer."

"We're not, but he's one of the reasons we aren't using flashlights. I'm hoping that blood we found today means he'll be laid up for a while."

"Long enough for me to figure him out anyway." She gave her temples a double tap with her index fingers. "There are more than a dozen disconnected details flitting around in my brain, like puzzle pieces I can't capture long enough to fit together."

"It'll happen." Setting his hands on her waist, he helped her scale a craggy rock wall. "Twenty feet, and we're there."

It was an optimistic assessment, but she made it—and only scraped one palm in the process. She noticed that Logan wore a shoulder holster with his two-way radio attached to the upper strap. So much for any romantic notions she might have been harboring. Both his manner and his equipment said he was on duty tonight.

From the top of the ridge, she made out the shadowy sprawl of a farm below.

Logan shed his pack in a patch of soft scrub and grinned at her. "You're straying awfully close to the edge, Sera."

"Am I?" But she didn't back up until he hooked a finger through her belt loop. "That's the Bulley house, isn't it?"

"You have good eyes."

She indicated a collection of lights about a mile to the right of the dilapidated structure. "That must be the campsite for the project workers." She also spotted a rickety barn, a ramshackle collection of outbuildings, a large pond and several patches of black woods. When something fluttered in her peripheral vision, she found herself smiling. "You brought a blanket?"

"Can't have a picnic without one." He spread it on the scrub and tugged her down beside him. She sensed he was as surprised as she was when his fingers wrapped around her neck and his mouth came down on hers in a kiss that chased away any hint of cool in the night air.

Although she could have taken it a lot deeper, suspicion had her drawing back. "I know you, Logan. Much as I'd love to, I don't think you brought me up here to have wild sex under a nearly full moon."

"You don't have a very romantic vision of me, do you?"

"Oh, I have many naked visions of you. But sometimes, like now, you're not."

"You think naked's romantic?"

Catching his T, she gave him a hot kiss. "Look in a mirror, Chief. You'll figure it out. Meantime," she ran a finger around his radio, "I think I can answer my own question. I had a chat with Benny Bulley today. He was wasted. He'd also been bitten by a leghold trap."

Logan chuckled. "What did he tell you?"

"He insists someone moved the traps. Not far, just out of the way. Of what, he wouldn't say, but he mentioned trespassers and that his grandfather fired off several rounds of buckshot when he spotted a group of them sneaking through the woods toward the ravine. I believe he called the spot Dilly's Drop."

"Dilly was his grandmother. It's not a pretty story. Go on."

"Old Edgar claims the farm and a few of his relatives' homes in town have been burgled more in the last week than they have in the past ten years. You'll be pleased to know, he doesn't hold any of that against you, but he's starting to wish he hadn't rented his empty pastureland to Abe. On the flip side, Benny says he and his brothers can deal with the trespassers from now on, so you shouldn't worry your head about it."

"Man's a prince."

Spotting a light below that hadn't been there earlier, Sera followed Logan's lead and got down on her stomach. "What?" she asked when he removed a pair of binoculars from his pack. "Is it a Bulley?"

"No. Someone's leaving the workers' campsite and heading for the ravine." He shifted the glasses. "There's a light in the old Morgan house."

"Is that bad?"

"Probably kids smoking up."

"Or making out."

"You think that, you haven't seen the old Morgan house."

Reaching up, she altered the trajectory of his glasses. "The first light's closing in on the ravine."

"Apparently the guy behind it is unaware that the last of the Bulley boys was released this afternoon."

Sera rested her weight on her forearms. "They have another still down there, don't they?"

A smile touched Logan's lips. "They have two. One in the ravine—which accounts for old Edgar's buckshot—and a second in the outhouse. Danny and Lester pulled their knives this afternoon and went after a couple of guys from the work site who swear they were only trying to use the thing."

"Don't you just love a bad lie?" She borrowed his binoculars. "Question, Chief. Gross out-house aspect aside, if the Bulleys are going to keep building stills regardless, why don't you let them have one? Control's in your camp then."

"Because they don't drink everything they brew. They sell more than half of it."

"Well, yes, but… Ah, right. They sell to anyone with cash, including minors." Her brow knit. "I can't believe Edgar would condone that."

"He doesn't. Unfortunately, Edgar and his grandsons don't subscribe to the same moral code."

"So what's the next move?"

Logan shrugged. "We wait. We eat pizza. We don't get sidetracked."

"Well, you're no fun."

Cupping her nape, he turned her head to kiss her long and deep. "Wanna say that again?"

She grinned. "You're no—" the amusement

faded "—ghoul," she finished slowly and with a frown. "That's so weird."

"You're telling me."

"No, really." She went through it in her head. "As the Blindfold Killer was running toward me, I'm sure he said something about a grave and a ghoul."

Logan's two-way radio squawked. "Something?" he asked.

"I've got a pair of Bulleys heading for the ravine," Fred's voice crackled back. "Should we move in?"

"No, let them go. They'll threaten whoever wants to steal their hooch, but they won't hurt him. Jail cell'll still be fresh in their minds."

"If you say so." His disappointed deputy signed off.

Logan's gaze held steady on Sera's. "Anything else?"

"If I'm a ghoul for witnessing a murder, I'm a ghoul who loves pizza and a movie. Already got the pizza." She tapped the thermal box, then indicated the light now retreating quickly back to the campsite. "I can't wait for the feature presentation."

LOGAN'S PATIENCE AND timing amazed her. Two pieces of pizza and a brief surveillance later, he had the Bulley boys plus their grandfather lined up, fined and grumbling in resigned frustration.

"You'd think they'd learn." Fred followed Sera up the back porch stairs to the house. He waved a hand to activate the light sensor. "Flo and Babe play bingo twice a month," he explained. "That's why the place is dark."

So either their daughter was upstairs sulking, or she'd gone out for the evening. Fifty-fifty either way, Sera figured.

In the kitchen, Fred exhaled. "Guess I'll have a look-see for Autumn. Logan said he'd be home inside half an hour. Kinda wish he hadn't kept Ella, but she's good at sniffing out hidden whiskey barrels. Do you mind being housebound for a while, Doc?"

Sera plucked a twig from the tip of her pony-tail. "All I want to do is take a bath, sing Bob Marley and think about ghouls and tan lines. Don't ask," she said at her companion's perplexed expression. "Just be happy you've never been hypnotized."

Fred trudged up to the third floor while she nabbed a bottle of cold water and started toward her room.

Except it wasn't her room, it was the guest room. Logan's guest room, in Logan's house. It hadn't taken her long to stake a claim. It had taken even less time to fall...

She halted with the bottle raised to her lips. "Whoa, okay, back up, Sera. You don't know what you're feeling right now. Think in maybes, not certainties."

But that was the shrink in her talking, and the further she strayed from that particular branch of medicine, the cloudier she became about going back.

Did those clouds mean she loved Logan, or

that she only thought she did because of circumstances and proximity?

Taking a drink, she continued walking. All in all, she'd be better off pondering ghouls and graves and speculating on why a killer had been uttering words like that as he'd run toward her.

She needed to go through the night again, frame by frame. She could thank Hollis for making that much possible.

A protracted creak of floorboards from above brought a smile to her lips. Glancing at her scraped palm, she released her ponytail, rearranged her cap and started to hum.

The moment she did, the killer burst through her office door, charging toward her, coat flapping. No—she held herself perfectly still—not a coat, not exactly. It was a three-quarter-length protective work jacket, the kind the maintenance people in her office building wore.

She stared at the corridor wall, careful not to rush the memory.

The mothball and mildew smell struck her

strongly. The words he shouted echoed and overlapped. He wore a watch. Then, in a blink, he didn't. There was only a tan line. Same man, she realized, two looks. And the smell was gone, too.

"'He's dead, in his grave,'" the killer raged. "'No one puts a ghoul in his grave…'"

She frowned. That couldn't be right. But she sensed it was close.

When the image went irretrievably fuzzy, she opened the door to her room and went inside. An unexpected movement near the bathroom snapped her into the moment. Swearing, she spun and shouted automatically.

"Fred!"

Awkward hands grabbed her from behind. She tried to turn but couldn't, so she jabbed an elbow into her attacker's solar plexus and used her heel on his foot.

A stiletto would have been better, but the hiking boot worked because he yelped and thrust her into the wall.

Something hit the floor. He gave her another rough shove.

"Fred!" When he yanked on her hair, anger overrode fear. "Bastard," she hissed and groped for the table lamp.

As her fingers curled around it, she wrenched herself out of his grasp just enough to swing the base like a bat. She'd been going for his head, but the strike on his shoulder did the job. He tossed her into a small table and went for the partly open door.

Stairs creaked. She heard footsteps in the hall. Feet pounded. Then everything stopped.

"Fred?" Running across the room, she set a hand on the doorframe and swung out. Giddy relief swept through her. Not Fred, she realized, resting her head on the wood, but Logan.

It had to be mild hysteria that made her want to laugh. Logan had a knee planted in her attacker's back and a hand clamped around his neck.

Letting out a deep breath, she asked, "Who is it?"

"Old barmate of ours."

When he dragged the man's head up, her eyes widened and the laugh escaped. "Are you serious?"

There, lying on the floor, with one of her purses wrapped around his arm, was the biker Logan had ticketed several days earlier—Wayne Postle.

"So it was Wayne who jumped me in your room the night the power went out."

"The night it was cut." Logan handed her a mug containing the dregs of the day's coffee. "For the record."

With a doubtful glance at the contents, Sera braved a sip. "This is the second time he's assaulted me then. That pisses me off."

"You're not alone."

Smiling at his dark tone, she pushed the mug back into his hands. "Your coffee's terrible."

"Toby makes it."

"From the by-products of an outhouse still?" she countered sweetly and made him chuckle.

He was on station duty for the remainder of the night, thanks to Annabelle's in-laws who'd shown up unexpectedly for Blue Ridge Days. After bringing Wayne in, Logan had cut her loose and sent his night deputies out on patrol.

Sera poked a finger into the soil of a withered cactus. "Talk to me, Chief. Who did what the night Wayne blindsided me in your room?"

"Wayne is Autumn's boyfriend."

"What?" Astonishment halted her halfway to the sink. "Did Wayne tell you that?"

"He didn't have to. She had the keys to his Kawasaki in her pocket the night she crashed Flo's car into the barn. That's why she took off in the first place. To rendezvous with him. She met him where he'd been holed up—in a work shack on the Bulley farm. He used the shack both as a flop and as a storehouse for everything he's stolen since coming to Blue Ridge. It's a sizeable stash, and it explains the recent rash of thefts."

"About which I'm guessing you already had your suspicions."

"What can I say? He fit the profile. As for the night in question, the Bulley boys were all in jail, and Wayne, being an opportunist with a nose for hooch, saw the still he'd been fortunate enough to stumble across in the ravine as a liquid gold mine. He and Autumn went there, swiped a couple quarts and got wasted. He passed out, and she drove back home."

"Via the barn. She kept saying 'Dumb hick' while I was putting her to bed. She must have been talking about Wayne."

"Yeah, well, first he kept her waiting, then, when he finally showed up at the shack, she discovered he was out of commission for the night thanks to you."

Sera filled a small watering can and cast a smile over her shoulder. "I'm jumped, I fight back. So you're saying they got drunk after Wayne broke into your house."

"Call it a medicinal bender." Logan dumped the cold coffee and rinsed the mug. "Far as I can tell, he wasn't sure if Autumn was there or not when he arrived at my place. She wanted to keep their relationship quiet, so he skulked around outside, saw you and Flo in the kitchen and decided to climb up the trellis to my room."

Sera gave the cactus enough water to soften the soil. "So we know Wayne's inside the house. Can we skip to the Blindfold Killer?"

"He probably used the side door. Flo's mind's been tied up with Autumn, and until recently, she hasn't been turning locks."

"Oh good, more guilt."

"Why? Because you witnessed a crime? Screw that, Sera. The guy got in and got lucky. The breaker box is right inside the door. He must have flipped off the house lights thinking it would be easier to dispose of you in the dark. Flo came in. He whacked her and went after you. But you had a weapon, and his balls, while expanding, aren't that big."

Boosting herself onto a cabinet, Sera let her eyes sparkle. "See what happens when you hang out with a shrink? You start analyzing every little thing."

"'Little' being the operative word here."

"You think the more people he murders, the more inflated the killer's ego is becoming, don't you?"

"Don't you?"

"I see an insignificant individual with grandiose dreams. Or maybe I should say a grandiose goal. He kills once—there's a weight off his chest. It can be done. Kill again, that's affirmation. With each successive death, his confidence builds. He goes in, bang, slash, stab, he gets out, fist pumped. Yes! He's got a signature, but he's a phantom, a fearsome one. Achieving his goal's gonna be a piece of cake. Then, uh-oh, sudden glitch. Not so easy this time around. But it's fixable. He has to back up, think the problem through, revise his plan, first with me, then, on the spur of the moment, with Flo."

"Revised plan fails," Logan continued. "One glitch leads to another. Maybe he's rushing. In any case, he's inside the house now. Power's out, Flo's a non-factor. He's back on track."

"Except—woo—I have a gun. I might fire, could get lucky. Then, dammit, Flo wakes up, finds me. But he's still got the dark and, for the most part, the upper hand. Flo and I go upstairs. No problem. He'll follow, kill us both. But, double damn, he spots headlights on the road leading to the house. Gotta be the police chief. Time to leave."

"He who fights and runs away, Sera."

"A sentiment the Blindfold Killer apparently shares with Wayne."

"You and Flo came into my room. Wayne panicked."

"He ran for the door, heard you, reversed and took a header out the window."

"Roared off on his bike, rendezvoused belatedly with Autumn, then drowned his pain and frustration in Bulley whiskey."

"Didn't learn any lessons in the process, but that's hardly surprising." Hopping down, Sera started toward him. "Do you think the killer and Wayne knew about each other?"

"I doubt if their paths crossed, although from what you've told me, Wayne might have heard the murderer taunting you. If he did, I'll get it out of him."

She didn't doubt it. However, at that moment, she didn't care. Or more accurately, she cared about something else and no longer wanted to think about thieves, murderers and or any person not standing directly in front of her.

Logan had a sofa in his office—not large, but adequate. Only a third of the station lights were burning, his night deputies were on patrol and the street outside was empty.

Drawing closer, she unbuttoned her black shirt, teased him with her movements. "Your prisoners are asleep. I can hear them snoring through two closed doors. You won't get anything out of Wayne tonight, and, although that pizza was good, all it really did was put an edge on." At his unreadable expression, she widened meaningful eyes. "My appetite." She walked her fingers up his chest. "Anything you can do to help me out there, Chief?"

He didn't say a word, just hauled her against him and crushed his mouth to hers. His eyes were glittering when he raised his head. "Answer your question, Doc?"

It might—if she could remember what it was. Every thought in her head had just been blasted apart. Only a shimmering haze remained—and somewhere in the nether regions of her mind, Bob Marley crooned softly.

Rather than fight it, Sera used the hypnotic rhythm to her advantage. She swayed into Logan, slid her arms around his neck, reached for his mouth. And only smiled when he swept her up in his arms and started for the back room.

Forget dinner in a fancy restaurant. This topped food by a landslide.

Poker debt paid in full.

HE COULDN'T NURSE his gunshot wound properly. He'd been forced to suck up the pain, drive into town, park on a side street and take a stiff-legged walk out to Main.

Had it been good luck or bad that he'd come around the corner at that particular moment?

The town had been in an uproar—people hammering and drilling, others on ladders, hanging flags and baskets and colorful ribboned signs. It had been an easy enough matter to secrete himself behind a stack of crates, but what he'd seen caused him to break out in a cold sweat.

What were the odds that this would happen?

He'd breathed slowly to calm himself. Odds didn't matter. The worst had transpired, but he was still ahead of the game. Of equal importance, he was ahead of the Blue Ridge police chief. He hoped.

What should he do? What could he do?

Don't panic for a start. Think, calculate, rectify.

He'd stood there, sweating like pig. And then, not half a minute later, a possible reprieve.

He'd looked around the crowded street. Busy, preoccupied people rushed every which way. It could be done. It must be done.

Relaxing his muscles, he'd pulled his hat down over his face, stuffed his hands in his pockets and wandered through the crowd toward the clinic.

Chapter Eighteen

"You're looking mighty pleased with yourself, Logan." Fred clomped into the station at 7:00 a.m. "Night crew punched out yet?"

"Half an hour ago." Feet propped, Logan examined the barrel of a rusty Winchester. He read the crudely carved initials and grinned. "Looks like we recovered Edgar's daddy's rifle."

"Part of Wayne Postle's loot?" Fred inspected the collection of stolen merchandise Logan had spread out over three desks and the floor. "Aw, what's this? He stole ladies' purses? What's the matter with him?"

"He was after the contents, Fred. You saw him with two of Sera's bags last night."

"And my silver dollar collection, and Sig's autographed Mickey Mantle baseball, your laptop, Sera's pretty diamond earrings and two tins of Flo's chocolate chunk oatmeal cookies that she baked for the potluck picnic raffle."

Setting the rifle aside, Logan swung his feet down. "Guy's in jail and loot's been recovered. We'll have a list of stolen items posted around town by noon. We dismantled two more stills, and Annabelle's in-laws have decided to stay at the hotel instead of her place. All in all, I'd call it a good night's work."

Fred tapped the side of his nose. "You and Sera've got something going, haven't you? I know it's…"

"None of your business." Logan glanced at the clinic, considered for a moment, then returned his gaze to the desks. "I've got most of this stuff sorted. All you have to do is tag the items and post the list."

The big man deflated. "Logan, about my kid…"

"She's an accessory after the fact, Fred. Get her into rehab, and stop beating yourself up. Autumn's getting a second chance. What happens next is her choice." He reached for his ringing cell. "Logan."

"I've got the lab report for you, Chief," one of the deputies from Casper said. "We e-mailed the results, but I thought you'd want the gist first-hand."

"And that is?"

"We brought up the breakdown on Hugh Paxton's blood work, then ran the samples you gave us and eliminated yours straight off. Left us with two. And point for point they're about as dissimilar as blood types get. Read into that what you will, Logan, but one thing's sure. I don't envy you your job right now."

A DOZEN CREAM-COLORED roses laced with baby's breath were waiting for Sera when she arrived at the clinic. They were artfully arranged in a clear glass vase and stood front and center on the reception desk. The attached card read:

Sera,
    If I am where I'm meant to be,
    Then where are you?
    Logan.

The cryptic question, not to mention the gesture itself, would have occupied Sera's thoughts all day if she hadn't gone into the second examining room and discovered the contents of a dozen or more patient files strewn across the floor.

Her first thought was that Dr. Prichard had let himself in and flung them from the cabinet where they'd been stacked. Her second was that 8:00 a.m. had come and gone and Beth, who'd promised to open the doors promptly at 7:30, still wasn't at her desk.

When she hadn't appeared by 8:30, Sera called both her home and her cell—and got no answer on either phone.

Nudging a curious Ella aside, Toby crawled around on his hands and knees. "If you're right, Doc, Prichard must have had some kind of mad on to do a thing like this."

Wearing jeans and a pale-blue halter-top, Sera took advantage of the early morning lull and joined him. Still unsure about Beth, she sat on the floor next to the alley exit and began sorting.

Her hair remained damp from the fastest shower she'd ever taken. Logan's fault, of course. They'd made love twice on his lumpy office sofa. When the night patrol returned, they'd driven to his house to rush through one of Flo's hearty breakfasts, change clothes and somehow pretend they'd gotten at least an hour of sleep last night.

Reaching over, she felt for the door beside her. If it hadn't been ajar and stuck, she might not have noticed the tiny scratches around the lock. But she did notice them—and didn't like what they implied.

Kneeling, she studied the marks. "Uh, Toby? Does Dr. Prichard still have his keys?"

"Mayor says we can't take them away until he's officially dismissed or quits."

A chill feathered along her spine. "In that case, we need to get Logan over here. I have a feeling it wasn't Prichard who went through the files last night."

HE DIDN'T LIKE the way the nurse scrunched her mouth and wouldn't look at him. The whole left side of his body throbbed like a bad tooth, and no matter how dire the circumstances, she was supposed to be a caregiver.

Abandoning discretion, he showed her his wound. "It's infected, isn't it?" he demanded.

She glanced up, then back down. "Judging from the ooze and the swelling, I'd say yes. But then I haven't got my glasses, and I didn't sleep very well last night."

He ground his teeth. "You took an oath to help people."

Her voice was quietly spiteful. "Nurses make vows, doctors take oaths."

"Fine, then I'll just kill you now and be done with it."

His lash of temper closed her mouth quick enough and actually made her lips tremble. "If you wanted me dead, you'd have killed me at my place. Not stolen my car and brought me here."

"I don't want you dead at all." Snarling, he hobbled back and forth in front of her. "The only person I'm after is Dr. Hudson. This is about justice, not how many corpses I can rack up. People stay out of my way, I leave them be. I'm not a homicidal maniac."

"Then why do you want to kill Doc Sera?" At his vicious look, the nurse dropped her gaze to the floor. "If you need medical attention, she's the one who can give it to you."

He would have laughed if a shaft of white-hot pain hadn't shot along his leg from hip to ankle.

A few pointy fingers actually kicked up into his chest and made him cough.

He set his face close to hers and drew strength from his fury. "Maybe I'll enlighten you before I'm done. Dr. Hudson might not remember what I look like, but she'll see me clear enough when I get her here." Whipping out a white bandanna, he gave it a snap. "I'm veering off the path with her. She's put me through hell, so I'm going to pay her back in kind. No easy death for her. I'm doing this for Papa. And trust me, Papa's really pissed off."

TOBY FELT CERTAIN it was one of his cousins who'd broken into the clinic, but despite the Bulleys' collectively vindictive natures, Sera wasn't convinced.

Whether Logan would have agreed or not became a moot point when a family of six rushed through the front door, shouting for her to help their grandfather.

The seventy-six-year-old man was having chest pains. His terror spawned a panic attack in his wife and caused his daughter to hyperventilate. Sera dealt with the most serious problem and was forced to leave the other two patients to Toby.

She thought he coped admirably, juggling mother and daughter and even thinking to contact the local paramedics for help. Unfortunately, they were out on a call. A five-car pileup ten miles south of town meant they'd be tied up for hours.

Sixty minutes flew by before she and Toby got things more or less under control. Then Logan's deputy, Walter, called to inform her that a pair of adolescents out four by fouring had rolled their truck. From the description, Sera suspected a broken leg and numerous fractured ribs.

She thought it was a good thing the old man's attack had turned out to be nothing more than indigestion. Still, considering it was barely 10:00 a.m., she foresaw a marathon day ahead.

MAYBE IT WAS the moon, Logan reflected, that was turning the town upside down. The pile-up on the Interstate had, as far as he could deter-mine, been caused by an angry wasp trapped inside the lead driver's shirt.

On the heels of that unholy mess, two boys who shouldn't have been behind the wheel, let alone scaling ridges in their father's Land Rover, had flipped the thing and gotten stuck inside. Fortunately, by the time Sera showed up, he and Walter had the boys free.

Five minutes later, Fred radioed with the news that shots were being fired at the Bulley farm.

Logan wasn't sure what he expected to find when he pulled up, but it wasn't Benny Bulley running out of the house in his underwear, shaken and clutching two knives. "Aunt Linda's gone nuts," he shouted. "She's got Gramps up in the attic, and she won't let him near the door." He lowered his eyes. "It, uh, could be she got her hands on one of our bottles."

Although he had weightier matters on his mind, Logan also had a job to do, and he trusted

Toby not to let Sera out of his sight. He had to believe she'd be safe until he figured out how to resolve the problem here.

He was rounding the front of his truck, running his gaze along the uneven line of old Edgar's roof, when the attic window shattered and a shower of bullets hit the rocky ground at his feet.

BLACK CLOUDS BEGAN massing over the Big Horn Mountains early in the afternoon. Sera noticed them, but because they didn't lighten the patient load or ease the nerves that had been fluttering in her stomach for most of the day, she put them out of her mind. They were clouds, she told herself, not portents of doom.

That she couldn't reach Beth bothered her. That Logan hadn't returned to the station by 3:00 p.m. bothered her even more.

Walter agreed to check on Beth. Twenty minutes after leaving, he called to say she wasn't home and her car was missing from the driveway.

An unconcerned Toby informed her that Beth had a number of quirky friends in Casper. He figured she'd simply received a call from one of them during the night. Toby's girlfriend, Beth's granddaughter agreed, but said she'd try to locate her once her shift at the post office was done.

Outside, the black clouds continued to gather over the mountains.

"People are hustling their butts to get the bleachers up," Toby remarked. "Word has it old Joe's predicting a bad storm."

"The weather channel said sunny and hot…" Sera moved a humorous hand from side to side. "But you prefer to go with old Joe."

"Absolutely. Another month in these parts, and you will, too."

Sera opened her mouth, then closed it and picked up a chart. "I have a patient waiting. Let me know when Logan gets back."

Ella padded obligingly from room to room. Toby manned the phones and did his best not to squirm when a rancher began describing his hemorrhoids in detail.

The clouds crept closer. The sound of hammers and power saws moved farther down the street. Sera was snapping off a pair of latex gloves when a familiar head with curly brown hair poked around the examining room door.

"Looks like you've got a bit of a break going on, Doc. D'you have a minute to look at my leg? It's burning like the devil."

She tossed her gloves in the trash. "You didn't step in a rabbit trap, did you?"

He rasped out a laugh. "Trap'd need to be two and half feet across to get me where I'm hurting."

Taking his arm, she helped him onto the examining table. "Is that blood on your pants?"

"Yeah."

Tight-lipped, he held fast to her wrist. His grip

was so tight she had to pry his hand free. "Hold on to the table," she suggested.

Thunder rolled in a single, ominous peal across the sky.

"Radio said sun all day," he noted in a rasp.

She smiled. "Guess the weather people forgot to check with old Joe. He's the local…"

She broke off as the tan line halfway up the man's right forearm slapped her like an open palm. Bob Marley began to sing. She was transported instantly to San Francisco. A man's hand squeezed her arm. He wore a scratched chrome watch—and then he didn't.

Back in the present, her eyes snapped up. And she saw him. Same face, same man, both in her San Francisco office and here in Blue Ridge.

Her patient's pained expression transformed into a slow, evil smile.

"And there it is," he said softly. "Recognition. You see now the person you saw then. What you don't see is what brought this about. But you will." His left hand whipped up to clamp around her throat. His right pushed the tip of a gun into her ribs. "Before you die, Sera Hudson, you'll see what it is to be helpless. And you'll know what it is to beg."

LOGAN DIDN'T ANTICIPATE a three-hour melodrama at the Bulley farm. But as a jittery Benny informed him, Aunt Linda knew her way around a thirty-thirty.

Apparently, she wasn't drunk. Edgar simply hadn't been giving her her medication.

"He said it was making her loopy," Victor revealed with a shrug. "But I say better loopy than loony. Good luck coming up with a plan, Logan. The attic has windows on every side. She'll see you coming no matter what."

Because he didn't have the power to become invisible, Logan opted to wait her out. But only to a point. When she showed no sign of backing off, he decided to call her bluff and go in through the front door.

Black clouds slunk in to obscure the setting

sun. He heard a trill of laughter as he stepped into the open. It didn't surprise him that she fired three bullets into the dirt in front of him. It didn't stop him either.

The laughter continued. The cloud cover thickened. Logan kept his eyes on the shattered window and his footsteps measured.

She fired again. And again. But she didn't hit him, and if her eyesight held, he didn't think she would.

Altogether, it took about five minutes to cross the yard and climb the stairs to the attic. The knob turned easily under his hand. With his gun lowered, he gave the door a shove—and held his position when she snapped the rifle toward him.

Motioning Edgar out, he forced her to focus on him. She tracked him as he circled the room. But there were no more bullets, and she offered no resistance when he wrapped his fingers around the rifle barrel and gently tugged it out of her hands.

For a moment, she simply stared. Then her face lit up, and she reached out to slap his shoulder.

"Well, hey there, Logan. 'Bout time you came calling." All smiles now, she pointed at a wooden tray. "Care for a cup of tea?"

"THIS IS WHY you're the chief of police and the rest of us are deputies." Fred clapped Logan on the back. "Damn but that was good."

It had also eaten up a lot of time, and Logan wanted to get back to town.

Leaving Walter and Annabelle to clean things up, he pushed Fred into his truck and answered his ringing cell.

"Yeah—Logan."

"Oh, hello," a woman replied. "My name is Jody Frost. I'm returning your call from last night. You wanted to know why I contacted Sera Hudson earlier this month. The answer is, because my sister's friend Kate was murdered… By the Blindfold Killer."

The hesitation in her voice wasn't something Logan could miss. Or ignore.

He started his truck and swung it around in a half circle. "You called Sera—Dr. Hudson on her personal line the night her colleague was killed, is that right?"

"Yes. I used a pay phone. Dr. Hudson answered and agreed to meet me. Of course that meeting never happened, but because it was her colleague who died, I realized I'd been wrong in any case."

"Wrong about what?"

"A possible connection between Kate and Dr. Hudson. Let me backtrack. I found Dr. Hudson's name and her work number written on a sticky note in Kate's address book. It had an arrow to another name—Harvey Gould. I don't know why I remember this, but a few years ago, Kate mentioned a man named Gould to me. Through a twisted sequence of events, Mr. Gould was removed from his home and put in a mental facility."

"Why?"

"Because that's where he needed to be. Kate didn't go into great detail about the case as such. She couldn't because it wasn't actually hers. Her part in it was more that of a bystander, a concerned citizen if you will."

"Concerned in what way?"

"It's a rather convoluted story. Suffice to say my hunch was wrong. You see, I thought what with Kate writing down Dr. Hudson's name, then drawing that arrow to Harvey Gould's name, then Kate getting killed, and, well, knowing how enraged Harvey Gould's son became after his father's commitment and subsequent death, that maybe he—Harvey Gould's son—might be the one who'd done the killing."

"You thought Harvey Gould's son murdered your sister's friend, Kate."

"Exactly. And if he had, then that would make him the Blindfold Killer. I know it sounds crazy, but it made sense to me at the time. So I called Dr. Hudson and arranged to meet her because if I was right, then she was in terrible danger. She was part of the Gould case, so in my mind it stood to reason. But as I said, when I heard about her colleague being killed, there went my idea.

"My sister told me to let it be. Don't dig into it on my own, don't contact the police, just go back to my day to day and leave the detecting to those best qualified to do it. I decided she was right. No one ever followed up, and I thought it was over. I was out of it. Until you called."

It took all of Logan's police training to keep his emotions in check. "What was the son's name, Ms. Frost? Do you remember?"

"Owen. Owen Gould." She gave a rueful laugh. "I don't know what made me think he might be a cold-blooded killer. I mean, after all, angry or not, he must have undergone some form of scrutiny before he was hired."

Logan's eyes narrowed. "Hired?"

"Yes, as a maintenance person. For the San Francisco Police Department."

Chapter Nineteen

The first thing Sera saw when the killer shoved her into the old farmhouse was Beth slumped against a crumbling plaster wall.

He'd tied her hands at the clinic and forced her out the back door into the alley. She had no idea what he'd done with Toby or Ella. She could only pray he hadn't killed them. Or Beth.

"Nurse isn't dead," he growled as if reading her mind. "Only sleeping."

He shoved her again, this time onto a rough wooden chair. "You don't remember me, do you?"

Sera swallowed as much of her terror as she could. "I do now."

"I don't mean from the clinic."

"Neither do I."

"Not from your office either. I'm talking about before that. Back when people started sticking their noses into things that didn't concern them." At her silent stare, he bared his teeth. "First his neighbor's niece got involved. Butted in even though her aunt had moved away by the time the shinola hit the fan. Then, there was that idiot insurance man. Any driver who can't see a twenty-pound cat in the middle of a quiet street has no business owning a car. And let's not forget the social worker, Kate Something, who was out of her jurisdiction but just had to interfere the day he suffered a little episode in the park. Did he ask for help? Did I? No. Just go away, lady. I can handle him."

"Him," Sera repeated carefully. "Who is he?"

The man's face reddened. "He is—he was—my father. The buttinsky niece insisted on talking to her aunt's soon-to-be-ex-landlord.

Landlord hemmed and hawed, but didn't do much except warn me to keep him quiet. Fine, I would. But then the social worker from the park tracked us down, said she felt duty bound to help. She talked to the landlord, who called the niece, who talked up a storm even though auntie dearest was living in Minnesota by then. Enter idiot insurance man who steamrolled companion cat and sent my father over the edge. I stepped in, told everyone to calm down and back off. It was just another episode. I'd get him a new cat. Things would settle down, so please, go away.

"But Kate the social worker wouldn't leave it alone. She was gonna help that delusional old man. Oh dear, did I say delusional? Enter medical doctor. I haven't done him yet, or the weaselly landlord, but I will because medical doctor led to psychiatrist, and psychiatrist led to my father being carted off to a hospital. It was supposed to be him and me, always, just the two of us, but suddenly there were people everywhere. Busybodies and do-gooders. Except my father died a month after he went into that hospital."

"But if that's the case…"

"Shut up," the man spat. "He died. Did the judge who put him in that hospital care? No. None of you cared, but oh, how you congratulated yourselves. Look what we did. We got a noisy nuisance the care he needed. Applause, applause. Too bad the old guy died, but that's not our problem. We did what we could, what was best."

The man's breath heaved with the force of his emotions. The hatred in his eyes burned right into Sera's head… And prompted a memory that feathered along the edge of her brain.

Something in the killer's expression and the semi-lucid story he'd related rang a hazy bell. About an elderly man in the advanced stages of dementia, who'd been admitted to a San Francisco hospital. About a medical doctor who'd called in a psychiatrist, who'd conferred and examined and agreed with his diagnosis. About a hearing, and a decision, and an ending that wouldn't sit well with many children.

The killer limped around her chair, shooting poison bullets with his eyes. One more look at his face and the haze cleared. "Gould," she exclaimed softly. "Your father was Harvey Gould. That's why you were shouting at me. *That's* what you were shouting. Not 'ghoul' but 'Gould.'"

A sickly layer of sweat coated the killer's face. Leaning over from behind, he grasped the back of her chair. "I made a vow the night he died. I'd cut through the red tape you wrap yourself in and kill all of you. I'd copy another murderer's MO and add my own special twist—I knew it would work because I knew the real Blindfold Killer's story. And I knew the story because I know how to blend in. I've been doing it for years. Insignificant maintenance worker, Owen Gould. No one really sees him."

"But where…?"

"Shut up," he shouted again. "I've come all the way from San Francisco to kill you. So make your peace, and be grateful for the chance to do it. It's more than your predecessors got."

A length of red tape and a white bandanna landed in her lap. His breath rasped in her ear. "It's all about details and using what you have, what you've learned. It's about shadows and determination and thinking on your feet."

The barrel of his gun grazed her cheek. Her shudder of revulsion drew a low chuckle.

"Say hello to the real Blindfold Killer when you see him, Sera. He's been waiting to greet you for eighteen long months—in the deepest pit of hell."

"I DON'T KNOW what happened, Logan." On the clinic floor, in the corridor between the washroom and the waiting room, Toby rubbed the back of his head. "I was walking and thinking how finally there was no one but me and the doc in the building and that maybe we could close up soon. Then, bam, everything went black. Next thing I knew, you were calling my name and I heard Ella barking."

Locking down his fear, Logan focused on the facts. The killer had shut Ella in the utility closet. He'd whacked Toby and God knew what he'd done with Sera. Or to her.

His stomach tightened into slippery knots. She'd been his target from the start. Killing her colleague had been a mistake. That's why the police hadn't been able to connect Andrea to any of the other victims.

Sera was the link—to the social worker and undoubtedly to all the others. For whatever reason, the police hadn't considered the possibility of an accidental victim. Neither had he.

Slamming the door on the worst-case scenario, Logan worked with what he had—not much.

There was no blood and no sign of a struggle. And no one on the street had noticed anything out of the ordinary.

He squashed the slimy tendril of panic that clawed through his restraint, and, although he knew it was dangerous, pushed his deputy for more.

"When did this happen, Toby? What time?"

"A little after five, I think." He clutched Logan's forearm. "Am I floating, or has the floor gone spongy?"

Setting his hands on Toby's shoulders, Logan checked the young deputy's eyes, then called to Fred. "Are the paramedics en route?"

"Three minutes," Fred promised. "Back door's open in Room Two."

"I know." He motioned to Annabelle who pressed a cold cloth to Toby's neck.

"I'm sorry, Logan." The deputy's eyelids drooped. "I thought Ella was with her, but now I think whoever took Sera must have locked Ella up while I was on the phone, then waited for me in the washroom."

A face formed in Logan's head. Portrait of the Blindfold Killer. A dozen thoughts swirled in behind it, but the face remained at the forefront.

He knew he could have reasoned it out, rammed it into some kind of order, but Sera was gone and time, if any even existed, was running out. All he had were those fragments of thought, his gut instinct and about five seconds to make a decision.

"Where do we start?"

Logan looked up at Fred, stricken and unmoving, wringing the clinic's handset. And went with his gut.

"Stay with Toby," he ordered. "I'm going after Sera."

"Where?" Fred waved the handset in a desperate circle. "You're hunting for a ghost."

"A ghost with a name." Standing, Logan checked his gun.

"But how do you…?"

Fred's voice died with the slam of the clinic door.

Thunder resonated overhead, a dark warning. But his sights were set on the name stamped in his head. Owen Gould. If the man had a driver's license, he'd have a face, and Logan would know who to look for.

All he had to do was figure out where to look.

"I CAN HELP you."

The words rushed from Sera's lips, a knee-jerk response to the gun now pointed in her face.

"You're bleeding. I can see you're in pain. Unless you want to risk losing your leg, you should let me take a look."

He jammed his gun up hard under her jaw. "Let you kick me in the nuts, you mean. Or stick a needle in that'll knock me out cold."

Sera's voice wanted to tremble, but she ground her teeth and spoke around it. "I don't have my medical bag, so no needles. The best I can do is clean the wound for you."

His breath hissed like a steaming pipe in her ear. "Your nurse gave me the names of some antibiotics. That's why she's still alive. I'll get them from the next town I pass."

"You won't be alive to take those antibiotics if that infection gets much worse."

He jabbed her with the barrel to emphasize his point. "No tricks," he warned.

"No tricks," she agreed.

"I'm not untying your hands until I've immobilized the rest of you. Twitch wrong, and there'll be a big red splat on the wall. Then I'll put holes in all four of your nurse's limbs and watch her bleed to death."

Sera controlled her breathing with difficulty. Keep him talking, she told herself. The clouds had created a premature darkness. He'd switched on two battery-powered lamps, and the windows had no shades. Someone—Logan—would notice.

"You help me, and I'll make it fast for both of you." He grimaced. "Screw me around, and your brain'll be the last part of you to hit the wall. You got that?"

"Yes."

Wiping his upper lip, he gave Beth a rough shake and ordered her to secure Sera to the chair with the roll of red tape he pulled from his duffel bag.

"Should I leave the knots loose?" the nurse whispered, but Sera shook her head. The killer was watching them closely, sweating heavily, trembling in spasms. It wouldn't take much for him to squeeze the trigger.

Buying time was the only chance they had. She had no instruments and no way of knowing what his pain threshold might be.

The bowl of water he made Beth set out looked murky and smelled like a swamp. The lamplight was bad, and her hands, although steady enough, had turned to ice.

"I don't kill for enjoyment," he bit out as he

bound Beth's ankles. "I only took Florence Nightingale here because I saw a certain patient going into the clinic yesterday. A minute later, I saw you come out with the redheaded deputy. Did you know, I wondered, or was fortune on my side? It took balls, I'm telling you, to stroll over and eavesdrop outside the door. But to my amazement, Florence was too busy to twig and you were gone, so I figured—I hoped—crisis averted. Still, I knew she made up the charts and the truth might hit her during the night. Potential result? Puzzled call to you or the police chief."

Beth's chin went up. "Lucky for you, it was a madhouse all afternoon. With Doc Sera away on an emergency call, I was run off my feet. I didn't have time to think, let alone sort through the new files. I left them on the cabinet when I went home last night."

"At which time I stole the one that mattered." His eyes glittered. "Then I came and stole you."

Considering her terrified state of mind, Sera was surprised the answer came so quickly.

"You used someone else's identity," she said. "You hung around the project work site and found the closest physical match you could. Then you injured yourself and came to the clinic under his name."

"Smashed my hand into a wall after the bar fight," he admitted. "Logan screwed me up, or I'd have had you that night. So scrap Plan A—it was on to the clinic. I knew I'd have to be clever. And flexible. If you'd recognized me, I'd have been forced to kill you on the spot. Not the best solution, but I figure I'm an innocuous-looking man. I'd have left town and blended back into the city easily enough.

"As it turned out, however, you didn't recognize me. I was able to take what I'd overheard in Gray Wolf's bar and use it to buy myself some time, get you all looking in the wrong direction. I actually presented myself to Logan.

I described Hugh Paxton just well enough that there'd be no doubt he was the man who'd tried to abduct you the night before. Then the helpful witness faded back into the shadows."

His mouth twisted downward. "You know what happened next. The worker whose name I'd used got injured and came to town for treatment. He's not a particularly sociable man. Still, I'd always known there was a risk my story wouldn't hold forever. Way I see it now, it held just long enough."

He gave the tape around Beth's ankles an angry jerk. "Chance after chance fell apart one way or another. It took me awhile, but I finally figured out why." He broke the tape with his hands.

Screwing his gun into the underside of her chin, he showed her his top and crooked bottom teeth, breathed his hatred through them. "I planned and I planned, and you messed me up.

You, your shrink friend, your so similar dark hair, your red coat, the rain."

Sera regarded him calmly, despite the metal barrel lodged against her windpipe and the fear scrambling around in her stomach. "You found him, didn't you?"

"Found who?" he demanded testily.

"The Blindfold Killer."

Beth sucked in a breath, but the man made a disgusted motion. "Of course I did. I worked at the police station, didn't I? And cops talk all the time. They jabber away, leave files open, go for coffee or to hit on the new blond dispatcher. What can an invisible person do?" The grin reappeared. Opening his shirt, he tapped the tattoo on his shoulder. "He can absorb and follow and if he's lucky, get where the cops are going first. He can use his luck and obliterate the very person he needs to fulfill his brand new mission in life. So long, original Blindfold Killer. Say hello to your successor, your shadow,

Blindfold Killer Two. Better than the first because no one will ever suspect him. They'll keep right on looking for Hugh Paxton. They'll look, but they'll never find. Because Papa's watching over him, and I watch over Papa."

"Doctor…" Beth began, but Sera kept her eyes on the man in front of her.

"You are a clever man, Mr. Gould. Attention to details explains why you've been so—successful."

He wiped his lip, then his forehead. "Messed things up with you, though, didn't I? You wore a red coat to work that day. It was dark. I thought it was you getting that take-out food. I forgot to check the face. But there's always a way to fix things. Papa fixed old clocks. He said there was always a way. And he was right. So here we sit, you, me and an innocent victim. Your victim. Your fault. Just like the detectives were your fault. And, of course, your associate. Never lend, never borrow." Both his features and his smile hardened. "Most of all, though, never mess with a madman's head."

In a sudden, vicious move, he caught hold of her hair. His mouth took an ugly downward turn. "That's what you're doing, isn't it, Dr. Hudson? You're trying to distract me, thinking maybe the kook will bleed to death and that'll be the end of it. But it won't be me who dies today. Clock is ticking, Sera."

Releasing her, he yanked a battered chrome watch from his shirt pocket and clasped it around his right forearm. "This was my father's. I wear it at home like he did and again when I'm avenging his death. I gave it to him when I was ten years old. Do you see the time? It says 7:20. That's when my father died. It's only right that you who caused his death should die then, too. When I brought you here it was 6:30. You've got less than twenty minutes to live, Doc. If my leg feels better when you're finished working on it, you'll die fast. If not..." He moved his mouth and the gun next to her ear. "Splat, splat."

RAIN BEGAN TO fall as Logan cut the flashers outside Abe's trailer. The builder met him at the door with a wave and a grin, both of which faded at Logan's dark expression.

"What? Am I under arrest?"

"Listen to your damn messages more than once a day, Abe." Logan shook the rain from his hat. "Roy Parsons. Get him here."

"Sure. Uh, any reason?"

"Yeah."

"Gotcha." Abe scanned a list, punched a number, told his assistant to hustle the man over. As the silence stretched out and the minutes ticked away, he lowered himself onto the edge of his desk.

Finally, he craned his neck and nodded at the window. "I told him to step on it, and he did… Get in here, Travis, and close the damn door before the rain shorts out my electrics."

Abe's assistant booted the door closed and, pulling off his hat, slapped it against his thigh. "Hey, Logan. What's up?"

The man behind him nudged his cap back, fingered the bandage on his cheek and appeared impressed. "Doc said this plaster'd stick, and she was right." Stepping forward, he stuck out his hand. "Pleased to finally meet you, Chief. Travis said you wanted to see me. Name's Roy Parsons."

OWEN GOULD TORE his pant leg open at the hip and positioned his chair parallel to Sera's. He planted Beth on a crate and stuffed his gun under her left breast.

"Move it, Doc," he advised gruffly. "I'm feeling woozy. I might have to abandon my plan and off the nurse here in one quick shot, save the torture for you alone."

Sera ordered herself to breathe, go slowly, stall without being obvious.

"This is going to sting," she warned and tipped some non-Bulley whiskey onto one of the man's wadded-up shirts—a shirt that smelled of mothballs and mildew.

"What?" he demanded when she rearranged it.

"Nothing. Too bulky. Are you ready?"

"As I'll ever be." But he turned a sickly shade of green when the whiskey met infected flesh. "Son of a..." He whistled in and out, then shot her a baleful glare. "You don't like it, but you recognize it, don't you?"

She raised her eyes.

"The smell," he barked. "Mothballs. I heard you say it in the bar, before I knocked you out." Moving his gun, he tapped the barrel against Beth's temple. "Details, Doctor. My father loved the smell. My mother hated it. She was a clean freak. Wash, dry, iron, hang." He gave a contemptuous snort. "Hell with that, my dad and me said. Wear it, toss it on the floor, dig it out when you need it. Mothballs'll cover any smell that needs covering. Powerful little suckers. And you remembered them, even when you didn't remember my face." Gripping the neck of the whiskey bottle, he took a long swig, his fifth in as many minutes.

The battery lamps were dying, Sera realized, and with them her hopes. Still, where there was light there was hope.

Rain lashed the windowpane. Owen Gould took another drink, then startled her by thrusting the bottle into her hand and leaping to his feet. He put two bullets through the chattering pane and fired two more into the rain.

"I know someone's there!" Livid, he bent over Sera's chair and wrapped an arm around her throat. "Untie yourself," he snapped. "Do it." He cocked the trigger.

She fumbled with the knots on her waist and felt the gun dig into her nape as she worked on her ankles. The second she was free, he dragged her to her feet. His arm was a steel band across her windpipe.

"Is that you, Logan?" he demanded. "Come out where I can see you, or your girlfriend's dead in five…four…three…"

Someone moved on the porch. A face swam into view. Not Logan's but Benny Bulley's.

Soaking wet and terrified, he gaped open-mouthed at the man with the gun.

"I was—looking for a new—a place," he stuttered. "I saw the lights and thought maybe one of my brothers beat me to it."

"Get in here." Gould jerked his head sideways. "Sit next to the nurse, and keep your mouth shut. I need to think."

He tossed Sera forward the moment Benny lowered himself onto a crate. "You know the drill, Doc. Tie him up tight, or someone in this room's going to take a bullet."

Sera knelt and picked up the tape Beth had used on her.

Benny's eyes went to the window but dropped to the floor when Gould darted a look at the shattered pane.

"Who else is out there?" he demanded.

"No one." Benny moved a foot. "My brothers and me don't travel in clumps."

Sera kept wrapping. Gould glanced at her repeatedly as he edged toward the window.

Benny moved his foot again, this time into her knee. "Not so tight, Doc."

Looking up, she watched his eyes and mouth. Rain gusted in, created puddles on the floor. Gould was sidling closer to the opening when his foot slipped on the broken glass.

As if someone had pushed a start button, the room came alive. Benny shot from his seat to tackle Sera. "Get down," he shouted and gave Beth's crate a kick that sent it flying.

A bullet from outside caught Gould in the shoulder. Reeling backward, he went for Sera, but she managed to roll away.

Roaring, he sent both lamps crashing to the floor. What light they'd been giving off immediately winked out.

Sera heard a moan. "Beth?" Unable to see, she stayed low. "Are you hurt?"

Hands shoved on her butt.

"Get behind the table," Benny whispered. "He wasn't supposed to kill the lights."

Gould knocked aside everything in his path. Bullets ricocheted off walls. Sera located Beth, but the nurse must have hit her head in the fall. She was groggy and only partially responsive.

"Untie her, Benny," she said, "and get her behind the table."

"But…"

"Where's your knife?"

"In my back pocket."

She reached around him and groped until she encountered the hilt.

"Everyone dies in pain," Gould ranted. He shot in all directions and from everywhere in the room it seemed.

Leaving Benny to splutter, Sera worked her way along the wall to what she hoped was Owen Gould's position. She estimated she was half-way there when another shadow moved and a hand closed around her wrist.

"Stop," Logan told her quietly.

Even as relief flooded through her, a bullet whizzed past her head.

"Logan, he's…"

"Shh." His fingers curled around her neck. "He's circling."

She gave his arm an urgent shake. "Beth and Benny."

"I know. Stay here. I'll draw his fire."

He was gone with the last word. Where, she had no idea. Until…

Above the approaching thunder, she heard bangs and grunts and shouts and finally a heavy thunk.

A body slammed into the wall directly in front of her. Gould's body, she realized. Her eyes had adjusted enough that she could see him shoving a new clip into his gun.

She didn't move, didn't twitch or even breathe. But somehow he knew. Before she could evade him, he reached down and tangled his hand in her hair.

"You die first, Sera Hudson," he growled. "At least I'll get that much satisfaction from this night. First you, then your bastard lawman lover."

As he started to yank her upright, Sera tightened her grip on Benny's knife. Double-handing it, she shoved the blade into his injured leg.

He howled in pain, dropping her instantly. She heard a single gunshot. For a moment, he didn't move. Then she saw his eyes widen and his jaw drop. To her shock, blood spurted from the center of his throat.

His gun arm swung around in a wild, drunken circle. He pointed it at her, but only for a second before his arm gave out and the weapon clattered to the floor.

"Should have stayed invisible," he burbled. And, head lolling, slithered down the wall into a motionless heap.

The physician in Sera had her crawling to where he sat, lopsided and staring. She pressed her fingers to the pulse point in his neck. When Logan came up behind her, she rocked back into him. "He's dead," she said quietly. "You're a good shot."

Setting his chin on top of her head, Logan asked, "Do you remember him now?"

She nodded. "Suddenly, I saw his face, my wet trench coat, Andi's body, all of it, as clearly as if the whole nightmare had happened yesterday."

He kissed her temple. "Yesterday's done, Sera."

While lightning flickered over the mountains, Sera let her tension slide away and savored the warmth of the man behind her. Through today and into tomorrow.

Epilogue

The story raced through town faster than one of Nadine's outlaw horses.

Benny Bulley lapped up praise for his participation in the showdown at the old Morgan farmhouse—even though his arrival mere minutes before Logan probably hadn't been as innocent as he claimed. Motive aside, however, he'd done what Logan asked. He'd clued Sera in by nudging her knee while she was tying him up and in doing so had earned himself and his brothers a free night at Tommy Gray Wolf's Bar.

The rain moved south, Blue Ridge Days opened with a bang—and, shortly after sunset, a minor brawl started between Victor Bulley and Abe's assistant Travis.

Abe apologized profusely to both Sera and Logan. The photo Logan had showed him of Owen Gould posing as Roy Parsons, although clear enough to most people, had been anything but to a man not wearing his much-needed glasses.

"It's all my fault," he moaned over and over again. Then he brightened as an idea struck. "Say, Doc, I'll bet your clinic could use some new equipment…"

Her clinic?

Sera might have corrected him if Jessie-Lynn hadn't tugged her aside to whisper that Doc Prichard had decided to pack up and move on. She claimed her alien friends had planted the thought in his head, and lucky for everyone in town, it had taken root.

As the night wore on, she watched men and women bid on their favorite picnic baskets at the annual Blue Ridge Days dinner auction. She watched Babe dance with Walter and a fully re-covered Beth do a jig with Flo. She made a point of not watching a patched-up Toby sneak under the bleachers with Beth's granddaughter.

She'd like to have spent more time—well, any time really—with Logan, but a moment here and there was the best they could manage given the demand for their attention.

Sera supposed it was only natural. Still, she wasn't sorry when darkness descended and the first starburst exploded in the clear night sky. With Ella nosing her leg, she edged backward across the street—and straight into someone's chest.

She knew it was Logan before she looked. Lips curving, she let her head fall onto his shoulder. "Hey there, stranger. Shouldn't you be busting Bulleys or getting hit on by every single female in town?"

"As tempting as those options sound, I'd rather escape for a while with one particular female."

A bottle of wine appeared in front of her.

"Sonoma Valley Cabernet." She ran a fingertip over the label. "Sig's favorite."

"He claimed the most worthwhile hangover he ever had came after a night spent with this stuff. I agreed with him—until I spent a night with some freshly distilled Bulley whiskey."

"Think I'll stick with the wine."

She heard the amusement in his voice when he lowered his mouth to her ear. "In that case, come with me, and I'll show you the best place in town to watch fireworks and get drunk."

Two minutes later, they were alone on the roof of the station house. Red, gold, silver, green and blue bombs burst overhead, filling the sky with jewel-toned sparkles.

Logan leaned against the rooftop door and Sera leaned against him. For a long time, neither of them spoke, just sipped Sig's favorite wine and watched the glitter rain down.

After awhile, she sighed. "Why does this feel so ridiculously perfect to me?"

"Probably because it is. Perfect moments

happen, Sera. They're rare, but not unattainable."

"Even when people you care about are dead?"

"Even then."

His simple response had her pushing off to face him. Setting her glass aside, Sera raised her eyes to Logan's shadowed face and ran a finger along the brim of his hat. "Sig told me you were the best chance I had to stay alive. He was right."

"You're the one who remembered his face, Sera."

"Yeah, two seconds before he hauled me out to his hiding place in the old Morgan house— which you also figured out."

"Lights on where they shouldn't have been—it wasn't hard to figure. Locals have more sense than to use that place for anything, and we already had Wayne Postle in custody. FYI, Postle did hear Gould threatening you the night the power was cut at my place, but all he cared about at that point was getting out before he got caught."

"Killers and thieves." She ran her finger from hat to cheek. "Different mentalities."

"Snakes and weasels." A smile touched his lips. "Different species."

"Gould was insane for a very long time, Logan, if he was ever sane to start with. He murdered the real Blindfold Killer. But you suspected that already, didn't you?"

"Crossed my mind. Gould was also the leak Sig talked about within the department. As for Paxton's body—no, idea."

"Ah, well, I've been thinking about that. You might want to check out his father's grave. If I'm right, you could discover that Harvey Gould is no longer alone."

"Sounds like you neglected to mention a few significant points in your statement yesterday."

Her eyes danced in the shimmering light. "Yesterday's done, remember? Today's just beginning and tomorrow's a magical mystery tour." She moved her hips against him. "Beth thinks I should give up psychiatry and stay right here in Blue Ridge. Recruit other doctors, expand the clinic." She drew a circle on his chest, set her tongue on her teeth, angled her head. "Anything you want to say to that?"

"No."

Undeterred, she bumped against him. "You sure?"

"Yeah, I'm sure." She sensed his eyes on her face and felt his thumbs slide along the line of her jaw. "Words are cheap, Sera. Action works better for me."

As his mouth came down hungrily on hers, Sera slipped the Sedona rock he'd given to Sig as a child into the pocket of his jeans.

* * * * *